Underground Glory

Dr. Horacio Sanchez

Dr. Horacio Sanchez

ISBN: 978-1-962624-61-9

3

In Loving Memory of

Hermann Nettel Lopez

Who left us too soon, but will never be forgotten.

Dedication

To my Daughters Constanza and Almudena

To Andres, you are my inspiration

To my wife Vera, this is a tribute to you

To Cecilia, Patricio, Fernanda & Family

To Friends and Family

To those who believe

To those who follow their dreams

Leaving a Legacy

Table Of Contents

About the Author

Dr. Horacio Sanchez is an Architect that also dreamed of writing. He began by publishing his first book about Architecture for Kids in 2017 and continued with the Architecture series publishing in subsequent years Architecture for Kids 2, Architecture for Kids 3, and Architecture for Kids 4, books dedicated to children interested in architecture, design, and art. Dr. Horacio Sanchez also published two books about supply chain and procurement. This is Dr. Horacio Sanchez's first fiction novel. A book that shows his evolution as a writer and his ability to transform his ideas and dreams into wonderful projects.

Chapter One

The ball merely touched the tip of Dena's spiky shoes, she felt the rubber skin of it brush against her big toe, and she instantly knew what to do. Everything around her dimmed out, and she entered her own sense of reality where she was all alone with the ball, the adrenaline pumping through her veins, the blood pumping against her skin; she became aware of every heartbeat, every breath, and every bead of sweat rolling on the side of her face. Instinctively, she flicked the ball to the right and easily dribbled past the first defender. She entered the goal box, the danger zone where she felt too much at home. She rolled the ball to one side and faked a dribble to the other as the second defender fell to the ground with his legs extended—it was a classic fake, something she had done too many times.

The goalkeeper was an easy problem to deal with. She easily chipped the ball over his head, and it landed straight into the goalpost. A hurrah of cheers went off, and it brought Dena back to reality. Normally she would never see herself in a social situation like this; kids cheering for her, chanting her name, patting her on the back, and telling her how she played amazingly as usual. At school, Dena was the person who preferred sitting in the corner of the lunchroom with her head buried in a book; it was not that she was a huge fan of reading per se, but the under cover of an old, dusty book, she did not have to interact with anyone she did not know. She was naturally a shy person. This is not to say that she was not sociable. In fact, apart from her conversational skills and social anxiety, she had a lot of things in common with the girls at school. She liked the same kind of music, she loved shopping for new clothes, and she was as trendy as them. However, to her, all these pleasures were private.

But not every person was as fond of her personality as everyone else. All Dena wanted was to be a regular girl. And she was a regular girl by all standards. But her natural introversion made her an easy target for bullies. For some of the senior girls, she was the favorite junior to mess with. This would normally happen during lunch hours. There she was, the fourteen-year-old girl, sitting in the corner, hiding behind the cover of her dark brown hair and an oversized book that covered her brown eyes, sharp-bridged nose, and rosy cheeks. Suddenly she would feel someone snatch the book aggressively out of her hands. She had stopped complaining at that point. She was far too aware of who it was.

"Well, well, well," said Cassandra, the brunette leader of the pack of three seniors that always walked together, "If it isn't my favorite junior!"

Dena just looked up at her and sighed.

"Can I have my book back?" she asked in her low, shy tone—she could not help that she always talked like that without meaning to.

The other minion spoke this time. This was Beth, or as Dena liked to call her, the "Rancid Red Head."

"Yeah, honey," Rancid spoke as she chewed on a gum, "You can get it back when you stop repeating outfits but we don't see that happening any time soon now, do we?"

Dena never understood what they got out of these little kicks, but she didn't dare complain. All she wanted was to get out of the situation as quickly as possible. So, she kept quiet.

Cassandra threw the book back at her, and she barely managed to catch it. Before they could leave her alone, she made sure to let in one quick jab.

"Let her read, girls," she said as she waved her hands, ordering her minions to walk away with her, "It's the only thing she has got going anyways."

The girls snickered again as Cassandra flipped her hair and walked away with her pack.

There were so many things that Dena had wanted to say at that moment. She also wanted to point out how rude Cassandra's attitude was considering how she was a senior, and she should be helping out kids younger than her instead of picking on them. Then again, she would have come off as more of a nerd than anything else, so maybe it was wise on her, after all, to stay quiet.

But there were times when she wished that she genuinely had the capability to speak up for herself more. She wished she had the ability to talk back to others and stand up for what she believed in, and make a name for herself. Her mind would often flash back to the time she applied for a position on the girls' soccer team at her school. She had excelled at the trials as she knew she would. She had no doubt in her mind that she would make it, and she did. Unfortunately, the seniors in the team seemed to have more say in the matter than she did, and she ended up being rejected because the captains decided that, unlike the cheerful, social butterflies that were bustling in the team, the girl who read a book in a corner in the lunch room was not fit to be in the team.

"You're just not ready yet," the captain had told her as she informed her of the decision. Instead of complaining, she just nodded and walked out of the room, carrying her paper of rejection in her hand and dumping it in the trash along the way. What the captain didn't know was that, unlike everyone else who played on the team for college credit and extracurriculars, Dena actually played because it was in her heart and soul. She had played ever since she was little. That is why she was a different person in the park as she played with her neighborhood kids. She had grown up with them, and she remembered playing soccer with them forever. She was a reserved person in front of them as well, but not to a point where it would affect her game. She could manage taking compliments and pats on the back from them. Plus, despite her social anxiety, it felt nice to belong somewhere. She would play until nightfall and then make her way back home to the suburbs, which were a ten-minute walk away. She lived in a small two-story home in small suburbia just outside of New York City.

Her parents did not mind her returning home late. In fact, they had always encouraged her soccer dreams. They wanted more than anything for her to become a professional soccer player someday. They had supported the dream ever since they had caught her sneaking into the living room, past curfew, and watching games of various European Leagues with her eyes glued to the television. Sometimes, however, Dena was not sure whether they supported her or just did not bother not supporting her. The thing is, her parents were always either too busy or too tired to look out for her all the time, which is why Dena had become used to fending for herself. It's not that they were never present. It's just that they never had a lot of time or energy to separately give to her. And Dena understood that more than well. She never held any resentment towards them. She understood where they came from and appreciated them for all they did, even if she sometimes needed more than she could ask for (at least emotionally).

Her dad, Frank, was a tall, burly man of 55. His retirement years were approaching, but he did not seem to slow down at all. He was the sole provider of the family, and he worked extremely hard for it. Despite her young age, Dena could see through his weary, tired face as he would step in every night into the living room for dinner. He worked 8 to 5 at a manufacturing company throughout the week. He was one of the senior managers there, so he would sometimes have to stay back in case of an emergency as well. People seemed to need him as much at work as his family needed him at home. One thing that Dena knew was that he was extremely selfless. It was not that he did not complain. It was not as if he was the perfect companion over dinner. He would complain about the most insignificant of things, as every dad did—the weather, the thermostat, the gas prices, grocery prices, the weather again.

But he was selfless in the sense that he woke up every day and worked without complaining to provide food on his family's table. No one asked him to do it. He just did it because he understood his responsibility as a man and a father. Her mother, Vera, on the other hand, did her best to cover up for her dad's absence. But being in a wheelchair for as long as Dena could remember did not help much with that either. Vera was a patient with multiple sclerosis, and, like any person suffering from MS, she had to make extra efforts to maintain her energy levels. Even performing the most mundane of tasks exhausted her to the point that she had to take regular breaks. Eventually, the muscle weakness and coordination issues got to her, and she became permanently dependent on a wheelchair. It took her a while, but the two wheels being dragged across the living room carpet soon became a functional part of her life.

When her condition had worsened a couple of years ago, Frank had stepped up instantly as he picked up an extra job to make up for her expensive medications and therapy. She had always felt grateful to have him and wanted more than anything to support him the way he had supported her. Recently, she started giving online Spanish classes to elementary school students. Frank had insisted that she did not have to put any extra pressure on herself. But she, as usual, rolled her eyes at him. Dena knew that despite him not being around the house much and her being tired all the time, her parents deeply loved each other.

Suddenly, the train of Dena's thought process came to a halt as she heard a familiar whistle.

"All right, kids," shouted Hank, the gatekeeper of the park, "Time's up! You kids better get home now."

One thing that was certain about old Hank was that he guarded the park with his life. No one knew why, but he just did. Dena always thought that he was one of those old souls who believed in principles more than anything. He was a thin African-American guy in his sixties who had chased the kids off the park after closing hours multiple times, but Dena knew that, despite his brash temper, he liked her more than anyone else there.

"Quiet kid," he used to call her.

The kids said goodbye to one another as they laughed and shrieked and made their way out of the park and onto their bikes as they headed home. They all waved at Dena from afar as she walked towards the other side of the park to fetch Lace. Lace was the beagle that had been in the family forever.

"Lace!" she yelled, "Come on, girl!"

The brown and white spotted dog with an unusually short-rounded body and small legs trotted her way to Dena as soon as she heard her voice. She bent down and received a wet kiss on her face that she wiped from the back of her hand. Lace yanked her tongue out as she panted slowly, and her ears drooped onto the ground.

"Aw," said Dena, "I missed you too, girl! Let's go home, come on."

They both made their way back to the suburbs. Dena didn't need a leash to guide Lace. She just naturally walked by her side. She nibbled on her chicken burrito as she walked at a slow pace. She was in no hurry to get home. Little did she know, her life was a couple of minutes away from taking a complete 360-degree turn.

Chapter Two

In Dena's mind, it was nothing but a usual evening.

She always entered her house from the backyard, where she would lock the gate behind her and untie Lace's collar. She would then walk up to the porch and take her mud-infested shoes off and shove them into the nearby shoe rack. She then slipped her socks off and tossed them into her bag. These would later go into the laundry basket along with the rest of her sweaty clothes.

This was her routine before sliding the key into the front door and gently pushing it open as she stepped inside. But today, there was something different about this whole ordeal. As she reached up to the front door, she realized that it was open.

"That's strange," she thought, "Mom never leaves the door unlocked before I come in…"

She shrugged and figured that she must have forgotten to lock it. But it was not just the gate that made her realize that something was different—and terribly wrong. It was the intense sobs that she heard as soon as she stepped inside that made her realize that something had gone horribly wrong while she had been outside.

All the lights were turned off as usual, and she could only see a dim light from under her mom's bedroom. That is also where she could hear the sobbing coming from. Her mom was a strong woman. Despite her condition, she had always been a motivational and upbeat person. She had always been optimistic about life and treated every day as a new challenge. Seeing her bright and charming smile every day, despite dragging a wheelchair across the house, had always been inspirational for Dena.

So it was more than unusual for her to hear Vera's intense crying coming from inside the bedroom. She was scared to open the door and see what was wrong. She reached the doorknob and gulped. She twisted it slightly and pushed it open.

She found Vera on the floor with her back against the bedpost. Her face was covered with her hands, and she could see tears dripping from the edges of her knuckles and down onto the carpet in a pool of what seemed to be a dark stain of tears on the red wool.

Her shoulders were visibly shaking, and in between the groans and the sobs, she took in small breaths and muttered something unintelligible. As Dena got closer and listened intently, she slowly started to make sense of what she was saying.

"Why? Why? Why, God, why?" muttered Vera over and over again.

Dena did not know what she could do. She had never seen anyone in her home cry before. Her father was a stoic character, and her mother was always the sunshine. But seeing her like this made Dena realize how truly depressing things could be had her parents been different people.

She managed to somehow reach out her hand and place it on Vera's shoulder. Vera flinched and peeped out of her hands and looked behind her to see Dena's round face staring back at her, concerned and anxious.

"Is…" croaked Dena, "Is everything okay.."

Vera just stared at her daughter's face, trying to think of the right words. Her lips trembled, but no sound came out. After a minute or so, she took Dena in her arms and started bawling. Dena could not understand what was going on, but she obliged and sank into her shaking arms. Somehow the tears got to her, and she could no longer control the pool that had formed on the edges of her eyes. She did not even know what was going on, but seeing her mother cry uncontrollably made her do the same.

"Listen," Vera managed to say.

"What is it, Mom?" asked Dena with her tear-soaked voice.

"Something terrible has happened…" Vera managed to say before her voice choked again.

She took a deep breath in and composed herself as she relayed the bad news to her unaware daughter.

"It's…" she managed, "It's your father…"

The tears swelled around her eyes again as she told her daughter that her father had been in a terrible accident. Her dad—the person who always kept his head down and made sure he did everything to provide for his daughter, the person with whom she never managed to have a conversation of more than thirty seconds, the person who grunted and complained but made sure he always did his duties—had died in a car accident.

Dena did not know how to react to what she had just heard. She could not comprehend the words coming out of her mother's mouth. Her vision tunneled as Vera's voice grew distant. She entered into a trance in the back of her head, where she was all alone, processing the news.

"Dad," she whispered to herself.

"It can't be…"

No one ever tells you just how stressful funerals can get, thought Dena.

She had been up on her feet all morning, attending to guests and paying her respects to everyone when it probably should have been the other way around. She had just arrived from the church and spread her father's ashes in the lake as he always wanted, and she and her mom were now serving food to the guests who had arrived from all over the city.

She had always heard that funerals were a dark and gloomy event, filled with sad clouds pouring down rain which mixed with the tears sprouting from the faces of the attendees. People gave gut-wrenching speeches, reminiscing about the lives of those who could no longer hear them, telling everyone how they had lived happy and fulfilling years.

If there was any sad speech or heaps of rain, Dena must have missed it because all she could remember since the morning was shaking hands with strangers and making sure they found the right places to sit as they told her how awfully upset they were and how they understood exactly how she felt.

How did she feel?

She barely had a moment to feel anything. All her energy was dissipated in greeting people she had never before heard of in her life. People whom she had never met or seen while her dad was alive. It all seemed hypocritical to her as she passed bread and tea to some old relative or the other.

Where had these people been all her life? If they were such close relatives and friends of her father, where had they been when her father was out working all night? When did they ever show an ounce of support to the family? Where were they on all the Thanksgiving dinners and Christmas mornings? She had never heard from any of them ever in her life. Yet, here they were, rubbing salt all over her wounds, having the audacity to tell her that they knew her father and that they could understand what she was feeling.

"Dena!" she heard a voice say.

She walked over to the living room to find an aging lady holding over an empty glass mug and waving it in the air.

"Dear," she implored, "Would you be an angel and take this back to the pantry?"

"Of course," smiled Dena as she took over the glass from her.

She walked back to the kitchen, where she found her mom aggressively cleaning dishes over at the sink. The sink was specially designed so that it was short and aligned perfectly with the height of her mom's wheelchair. It was her dad who had taken out the time on Sunday afternoon to redo the whole sink, which had now become a reminder of his love and presence.

Ever since the morning, Vera had thrown herself into all sorts of work around the house. She had been cleaning the rooms like a maniac before the guests had arrived, and once they did, she only took a moment to pay respects before she went back to making sure everything was perfect around the house.

Dena could not blame her, considering how she felt about everything she had heard since that Gow-awful morning, but she felt bad as she watched her wash one dish after the other, trying helplessly to throw the events of that day behind her.

She was trying to help out as much as she could. She even offered to take over the dishes duty for a while, but Vera snapped back, saying that she had it under control. Dena desperately wanted to sit her down and tell her that she was overworking herself and that she needed time to grieve. She owed that to herself. But she feared that having that conversation with her would turn into something aggressive, and she was not ready to deal with that, especially in front of the guests outside.

She gently placed the mug on the side of the sink and was just thinking of telling her mom to take it easy again, but she heard the kitchen door open and saw Aunt Fer walk in. Aunty Fer was one of the people she recognized at the funeral. She was one of her mom's closest friends and had also been one of the bridesmaids at her wedding.

She gestured at Dena to walk over to her. She opened her arms wide and gave her a warm hug, and planted a soft kiss on her forehead.

"How is your mom holding up?" she whispered in her ear.

"She won't stop working," replied Dena.

"Yeah," said Aunt Fer, "And what about you? How are you holding up?"

"I'm fine," lied Dena.

Aunt Fer was unconvinced, but she knew better than to pester her.

"Well," she said as she pulled away, "I'm here if you need anything. Now let me just get your mom to leave the dishes and come outside for a while. See you, kiddo."

Somehow Aunty Fer managed to wheel Vera out of the kitchen and into the living room, where she was met with more condolences than she could manage. But Dena was glad that at least she had left the dishes alone.

After an hour or so, the guests had started draining out of the front door, saying their final goodbyes, never to be heard of again. It was almost sunset when only Aunty Fer and a couple of other uncles that Dena knew of were left. She found this opportunity to use the washroom in the hallway.

She was only washing her hands when she heard voices coming in from the hallway. She thought of letting whoever was outside know that the bathroom was occupied, but the whisper of the conversation stopped her from saying anything.

It was her mom talking to one of her uncles.

"So, what have you thought about the house?" he asked her.

"Well, you know I can't look after this entirely by myself, and we obviously can't keep up with the expenses and all," Vera replied.

"I gave you my realtor's number, though," he continued, "Please give it some thought, okay? It's for the best. For you and Dena…"

"…at least that way, you'll also be close to me, and I could take care of you guys. I owe that much to the man…"

"Yeah," replied Vera dejectedly, "I know, but Brooklyn is such a big decision."

"It's still New York," he reassured her, "You'll fit right in, trust me!"

Dena gasped.

Had she heard her mom, right?

"Mom, listen to me, please," urged Dena.

"Look," said Vera, "I have heard enough, okay? I don't want to hear anything else. Just help me with all of this, okay? I am very tired already."

"Mom, please," insisted Dena as her mom handed over old cartons and tape to her, "I know things are hard for you here. But I'm here with you. We will manage…"

"Dena!" snapped Vera, "I don't want to hear this again. You won't understand all of this, okay? You're just a kid!"

Dena sulked as her mom put an end to the conversation.

It had been a week since the funeral, and the house was a complete mess, with everything taken out of its place, ready to be packed into a carton before the movers could arrive.

Dena's worst nightmare had turned out to be true. She had grown used to her neighborhood. If anything she loved in her life, it was routine. And her life in the suburbs screamed routine. But ever since her dad had passed, all the stability had shifted from under her feet. She was now packing her things with her mother, saying goodbye to the streets she had become too used to seeing and the faces she had grown up with. The saddest part of all was saying goodbye to the park, where she played soccer every day.

On any other day, she could not have cared less about her school and the people there (especially with people like Cassandra and her minions), but the thought of moving to Brooklyn and settling into a different, entirely new school was something that she could barely deal with. She had put that thought aside, knowing that it would bother her enough in its own good time.

She was just finishing packing the things in the living room when she noticed that she had missed something. It was a picture on the mantel of her dad holding her when she was a baby. She held it up and inspected it closely.

The tears pooled in her eyes all over again as she whispered to herself.

"Dad, I wish you were here…"

Chapter Three

It had been a while since Vera had stepped into a classroom and listened to the hustle and bustle of kids running around the place. On any other day, she would have considered it a welcome change, but considering how she had barely processed the events of the past month, the last thing she needed was to be around screaming kids all day. It was not that she was not fond of children. In fact, her years of tutoring had made her treasure the youthful preciousness that blinked gloriously in the eyes of children. She had grown accustomed to the chaos, the mischief, and the sly, innocent smiles.

Yet, despite everything, she felt outside of her element as she rolled into her cubical that afternoon. The move to Brooklyn had been tougher than she could have imagined. Not only that, she did not have a single moment's time of rest since she had to find a job as soon as possible. Just a month ago, Frank had been the breadwinner of the family. Her online tuition helped, but they definitely were not enough to take care of the entire household. Frank also worked from paycheque to paycheque, which meant that they did not have enough savings to manage for a couple of months while she worked through the chaos of their financial situation and the move.

Vera had no choice but to fill a teaching position at a kindergarten school near their Brooklyn apartment. Her disability was not something that came in between, thankfully, since the school was more than willing to accommodate her. However, she had been out of the physical teaching routine—waking up early for school, teaching kids in person, staff room shenanigans, grading papers, the travel, the meetings, and the bureaucracy—for a while now and fitting into the role was proving to be harder than she thought. With her present circumstances, she had no choice either.

Her job was to teach Spanish to elementary school kids, which in itself was also a relatively demanding job, especially since she was dealing with children. Her experience as a teacher had taught her that children demanded more time and attention than teenagers, whom she was more accustomed to teaching. She also had to change her teaching style in such a way that she could make a foreign language easier for her young students.

One would think that she would at least have the pleasure of unwinding when she came home every day after a hard day's work. As it turned out, stuff at home was challenging in an entirely different aspect—it demanded more mental energy than her job. She had to figure out a way to scramble through their crumbling finances. The apartment she lived in was not in a very nice neighborhood, and the owner had also pushed her to pay three months' rent in advance. She could have looked for other places to stay, but her budget was not very feasible.

She would come home every day to figure out ways to save money without cutting back too much on the necessities. She had a growing daughter to take care of, and there was no way she was going to let their circumstances come in between her well-being. It had only been a month, and the grocery bill, electricity charges, gas and water costs, and her credit card bills, had already piled up and were staring at her menacingly from the door of the refrigerator where they had been placed meticulously under the weight of magnets.

The rent was absurd, considering the place they had moved into was small and shabby. She had thought that moving into a small apartment would alleviate some of the costs of managing their old house, but, as it turned out, Brooklyn was expensive regardless of how shady one's neighborhood was and how congested their living situation was. The building they lived in was old and run-down; the stairwell creaked with each step, and rows of cracked wallpaper hung from the stained walls.

The apartment had two tiny bedrooms and an even tinier kitchen with moldy walls and a rickety floor bed. There was no internal heating, and buying electric heaters was out of their budget, so Dena and Vera tended to sleep in one room, covered with as many sheets and quilts as they could find. The small space between the kitchen and the bedroom doors was supposed to be a miniature living room, and it was occupied by a leather couch that the previous owners had left behind.

The only good thing about the apartment was that it was near Vera's workplace and Dena's school. Dena had been extremely accommodating throughout this trying time. Despite her age, she understood that her mom needed all the support she could give her at the moment, so she rarely complained and made sure to always be optimistic around her mom whenever she was dealing with the finances. She encouraged her to constantly look at the silver lining of everything. She was not sure if there was one in the first place, but she encouraged her to look anyways.

"We could be worse off," she would tell her every night over dinner.

The truth was, despite her cheery and encouraging attitude around the house, Dena was not doing very well herself. She had put a brave face around her mother and supported her as much as she could, but what her mom didn't know was how much she was struggling to fit in at the new school. Despite being unsure about the move, she was secretly glad to get out of her old school. She hoped to find better people, a fresh crowd. She was not so lucky after all.

Her introverted and closed-off personality made it hard for her to make new friends (not that she tried a lot). This also naturally made her a target, and she was often referred to as the "new girl." Her luck was not doing her much favors either since she soon found herself face to face with a new set of bullies who made life miserable for her in classes, throughout recess, and especially in the corridors where they would pass comments and occasionally shove and nudge her. She wanted to react, but she knew that she couldn't. Being the new girl made it hard enough, but she knew things could be worse off if she became known as the "tantrum-throwing" new girl. And so she endured quietly, just like she used to.

However, there was one thing that she was deeply excited about. The school had a soccer team, and the trials were coming up. She woke up extra early that day out of anxious anticipation. She had signed up for the trials and had promised herself that she would not only show her talent but make sure that she secured a spot. She reached school that day, and she barely paid attention to anyone as all she could wait for was the school to end so that she could stay back for trials.

She was tense as the final bell rang, and she made her way to the girls' changing room. She was surrounded by her batch mates and some seniors as they all changed into their kits. The room was crowded, so she had to wait outside while all the other girls changed. By the time it was her turn, almost everyone had changed and was stepping outside. She hurried into the lockers but looked back because she was sure that she had heard a couple of girls snicker as she went in.

"Wonder what that was about," she thought as she changed into her gear.

When she was done, she took a deep breath and reached the door. She grabbed the handle and said out loud, "Okay, I am ready!"

She turned the handle once and pushed, only to notice that it would not budge.

"That's strange," she thought as she tugged against the handle and gave it a harder shove. Panic settled in as she pushed the door over and over again, only to realize that it had been locked. It took her a moment to realize that someone had locked it from the outside.

"Uh oh," she said as the thought of the group of girls snickering when she went in rushed through her head. She could not believe it. They had actually locked her inside, and she was going to miss the trials. She eventually gave up and started screaming for someone to open the door, but no one came to her rescue. She spent more than an hour inside the sweat-filled locker room as she screamed and banged at the door. She started looking for some other way out, only to realize that there was only a single exhaust outlet there for ventilation, and she surely was not going to attempt crawling through that.

More than an hour had passed when she finally heard clicking noises from the door and rushed to it. She found herself face-to-face with a janitor who chewed her gum loudly and annoyingly asked her to scram. She grabbed her bag and made her way out as the tears started streaming down her face. The entire school was deserted at this point. The trials were over, and everyone had left. She walked slowly through the corridor but soon found herself sitting on the floor, her head covered with her knees as she sobbed uncontrollably.

It was not that she had missed the trials that caused her to cry in the middle of the empty corridor. It was everything. She could not understand how her life had turned upside down in just a matter of months. She could not believe how people around her could be so unnervingly cruel to her. She had not done anything wrong to anyone. She always minded her own business. She was also holding it together for her mom, and that took a lot of effort and energy.

She looked up from her knees and found her dad staring back at her, asking her to get up, telling her that it was all going to be okay. She wiped the tears from her sleeve, and when she opened her eyes, she found that she was alone again. She sighed and made her way toward the exit. All she wished for was for her dad to be there. As she walked back home, her shoulders slumped.

"Why do things have to be this way?" she thought, "Why can it not just be easy, for once?"

She suddenly broke out of her internal monologue as the voices of children playing and shouting entered her head. She lifted her head up and looked around. She noticed a park to her left. She had seen this park before as she regularly took this route back home. Only this time, it was filled with girls who, to her surprise, were playing soccer. She could not believe it. Girls playing soccer in the middle of the hustling and bustling metropolis of Brooklyn.

She watched as they passed and kicked the ball, and cheered each other up. She had not seen these girls at school, so she figured they must be from some other neighborhood. She was surprised she had not noticed them playing before. One of the girls kicked the ball hard in the air, and it crossed the fence and landed on the pavement close to Dena. One of the girls approached the fence and shouted.

"Yo!" she said as she waved her hands at Dena, "Can you throw the ball back inside?"

Dena smiled politely as she went to pick up the ball.

Chapter Four

It was truly astonishing how Dena had never taken notice of the park before. Despite frequently traversing this particular route on her way back to her apartment, the park had remained unnoticed, hidden in plain sight. Perhaps amidst the turmoil of everything going on in her life, she had failed to pause and truly appreciate her surroundings—the beauty that lay right there for her to admire.

From the moment she became aware of the park's existence on that fateful day, Dena made it her daily ritual to visit it after school. It was during those moments that the regular girls, whose faces she was growing familiar with from the pitch, would play their spirited games. The sound of the final school bell would spur her into action, dashing to the exit and sprinting all the way to the park, a temporary respite from her problems.

Seated on a nearby bench, Dena found herself engrossed in the game as it unfolded before her eyes. Sometimes the ball would stray outside the fenced area, and she would eagerly volunteer to retrieve it and effortlessly throw it back inside. This simple act had earned her recognition from the girls on the other side of the fence. To them, she was the quiet, new girl who came to watch them play, and they responded with warm smiles and friendly waves. For an introvert like Dena, it was a welcome change to have such friendly faces directed her way, especially after enduring a day full of bullies and dealing with the sandstorm of problems at her home.

The admiration she held for these girls grew with each passing day. Their camaraderie and chemistry on the pitch were evident, and they played with genuine passion and determination. It was clear that soccer was more than just a pastime for them; they took every aspect of the game seriously, from kick-offs to fouls. They even had their own dedicated referee. Observing them, Dena marveled at the mutual respect and lighthearted energy that permeated the air. It was as if they were one big family, laughing and supporting each other through the highs and lows of the game.

What impressed Dena the most, however, was something she recognized in just a few moments of observation. These girls were not merely playing for fun; they were serious athletes with a strong sense of commitment to their craft. Their talent and skills were evident, and Dena, with her own commendable abilities, appreciated the hard work and dedication that radiated from them.

As she sat on her bench, watching their brilliant performance unfold, she couldn't help but acknowledge the age-old truth: game recognizes game. Though she might be a bench away, Dena's connection with those girls went beyond words due to the common thread that linked them: soccer. Their mutual love for the sport formed an unspoken bond, and amidst the cheering and laughter, she found solace and inspiration in the talent that lay before her.

There was this one girl whom she had come to recognize as the unofficial leader of the pact. Not that the girls had a leader, per se. But she had come to realize that in every group in any type of social scenario, the same dynamic usually played through. This involved one person that everyone mutually accepted as the "decision maker" or "leader" of the group. This person was usually the most outspoken of them all and had everyone's respect and friendship.

Unsurprisingly, this group of soccer mates had one such person who stood out. After hearing conversations and banters, Dena came to the understanding that this girl's name was Constance but people just called her "Gio". It was a name she has not heard of before but it definitely had a nice and unique ring to it. She could tell from the very first day that Gio's energy reverberated through everyone on the field.

When she spoke, she spoke with defiance and sturdiness. Her voice could be heard all over the field as she shouted commands, yelling at her teammates to pass, shoot, or tackle. She spoke with a clear, high-pitched voice but her voice was one that did not ring in one's ear but was rather filled with clarity. But what stood out the most was, of course, her shiny, neon-green hair. She could be spotted from a mile away with those highlighted green streaks that reflected in an eye-catching contrast against the black roots of her head.

Green was not the sort of color that a lot of people went with when it came to hair dyes. This was mostly because a color as highlighter as green required a certain sense of confidence to pull off and not everyone possessed that. But seeing Gio demonstrate her top-notch skills with the ball and boosting everyone's energy with her commanding and persuasive voice, Dena could tell that she was definitely one of those people who were loud and proud about their green-colored hair. Dena could not help but admire her. Her personality seemed to be strikingly opposite to her own.

Gio would often catch Dena looking at her from the corner of her eye and she would turn to meet her gaze and offer her a warm smile. Dena would often look away in embarrassment and she would hear Gio let out a soft chuckle. Little did Dena know that one afternoon, after a particularly depressing day at school, Dena would find herself face-to-face with Gio and it would take the trajectory of her relatively mundane life in a different direction.

Dena was walking home from school that day when she decided to take her usual stroll to the park bench where she would watch the girl put on a display of their note-worthy feats with the ball. Surprisingly, the girls had not started playing by the time she arrived. They were only warming up. As they lay on the ground, meticulously stretching the muscles of their backs in yoga poses, she caught Gio's eye. She instinctively looked away, hoping that she had not caught her staring at her.

When she looked back, her heart started trembling slightly. She watched as Gio made her way towards the gate of the fenced field and walked outside. She was walking towards her. Her shoes were slung on her shoulder and they rocked back and forth as she strolled confidently towards her. She was barefoot but the raw pavement against her feet did not seem to bother her much. Dena internally considered making a run for it but she figured that she would look more of a wimp than she probably already did so she decided to stick around. She naturally had a tendency to assume the worst but, in that moment, she had no idea what Gio was going to say to her and how she would react.

Gio stopped right in front of her bench and made a short wave. She had probably sensed how tense Dena was from across the pavement and she wanted to let her know that she came in peace. Why wouldn't she? Dena replied with a meek wave and Gio made her way and sat next to her on the bench, a slight distance between them. For some time, she did not acknowledge Dena and just started over to the field where her teammates were stretching, apparently unaware of her absence. Dena figured that her teammates were used to Gio strolling around and making conversation with strangers.

After a while, Dena surprisingly decided to break the silence.

"I…" her voice was coarse so she took a moment to clear her throat. Apparently, all moisture had suddenly dried out from her voice box.

"I," she continued again, "I really like watching you guys play. You're real talented, you know?"

"Oh," replied Gio as she looked in her direction, "Us? Why, thank you!"

She smiled with a warm affection and that eased the tension in Dena's mind.

"So," asked Gio, "What about you? Where do you play? I mean, I know you play, that is for sure…"

"Huh," said Dena.

This caught her by surprise.

"You're not wrong," she replied as she eased into the conversation slightly, "But how did you know I play?"

"Because," Gio said as she smiled slightly, "No one spends their afternoon watching girls play soccer at a random park in the middle of Brooklyn. Only people who are actually dedicated to the sport do. And people who are actually dedicated to the sport are usually the ones who play. Am I wrong?"

"You're not wrong…" replied Dena as Gio's acute sensibility struck her by surprise. She got the impression that she was the sort of person who was good at reading situations. This is what perhaps made her a good captain on the field as well. But it also meant that she was the sort of person whom you could barely keep anything away from. She was the sort of person who could tell when other people were lying or hiding something from them.

She asked Dena where she studied and Dena told her that she was enrolled at the local public high school just down the block.

Gio raised her eyebrow and asked.

"So, I am assuming you play soccer there?"

"Ah," said Dena, "I wish. Or maybe I don't, I don't know. But regardless, I don't play there. Fact is, I haven't played at all since I moved to Brooklyn."

"You're not from around here?" asked Gio.

"I just moved from the suburbs," replied Dena.

"I see," said Gio, "I mean I figured that you weren't from around here but I didn't know you weren't a city girl."

Dena laughed.

"Is that a bad thing?" she asked.

"Not at all!" replied Gio as she bumped her on the side of her arm.

"So," she continued, "Why don't you play at your school again?"

"Well," said Dena as she took a deep breath in, "I am the new girl there, and the people there are not very accepting. So…"

She recalled the events of the trials and the thought shuddered through her skin.

"…let's just say I didn't make the cut," she summarized.

"That sucks," replied Gio, "Sorry about that…"

They both were quiet for a while then, comfortably sharing the silence.

"Well," said Gio, "Why don't you play with us today? We are one player short anyways. We usually are."

Dena's eyes suddenly lit up as the thought of playing soccer again, balancing the ball under the tip of her foot and sprinting through the boundless field, ran like a marathon through her head. She was also slightly concerned about playing with people she barely knew.

"Are you serious?" she asked.

"Of course!" replied Gio.

"I don't know…" Dena thought about it but she figured she would let go.

"Oh, come on," said Gio, "If you need shoes and a kit or whatever, don't worry. We have an extra one."

She really did not have much reason to refuse then so Dena reluctantly agreed. Gio delightedly clapped her hands as she grabbed Dena by her hand and dragged her across to the field where she hastily introduced everyone to her. Dena barely caught anyone's name as she hurriedly made introductions. The girls were all friendly so she did not have an entirely hard time adjusting to them.

As the game kicked off with a sharp whistle, Dena felt an electrifying surge of energy course through her veins. It had been more than two months since she last played soccer, but to her astonishment, she quickly regained her rhythm. The familiar moves of dribbling and passing felt like second nature, and she found herself effortlessly navigating the field, entering a state of flow where time seemed to slow down, and everything else faded away. It was as if she had stepped into a miniature heaven inside her head, where the only thing that mattered was the beautiful game unfolding before her.

A rush of pure joy engulfed her as she realized how much she had missed playing soccer. Each touch of the ball brought a sense of fulfillment that had been absent from her life for far too long. And now, in this very moment, that void was being filled, and her heart swelled with excitement.

Her newfound enthusiasm translated into action, and she scored not just one, but two incredible goals. The moment she sent the ball soaring into the net, a wave of cheers erupted around her. The girls from her team huddled around her, their faces beaming with admiration and excitement, and they raised their voices in jubilant celebration.

This experience was entirely new to Dena, and it felt surreal to be the center of attention and the recipient of such enthusiastic encouragement. In her past soccer games with neighborhood kids, they had come to understand her preference for solitude, opting to cheer her on from a distance, allowing her to bask in her achievements privately. But this was different. This supportive camaraderie and the sea of smiles surrounding her made her feel like a cherished member of a tight-knit team.

Dena was taken aback by the warmth and acceptance she felt from these girls. It was as though the game had not just revitalized her love for soccer but had also opened a door to a world of newfound connections. In this moment of triumph, she couldn't help but wonder if this was the start of something beautiful—a journey where she could fully embrace her passion for soccer while also forging lasting bonds with like-minded teammates.

The months of absence had done nothing to diminish her skills, and if anything, they had only reignited the fire within her. As she soaked in the cheers and encouragement, she felt an invigorating sense of belonging, knowing that she had found her place among these spirited girls who shared her love for the beautiful game.

By the time it was sunset, the girls decided to head back home. Surprisingly, Gio was walking back in the same direction as Dena so they decided to walk together. As they walked back, Gio asked her all sorts of questions and Dena replied as animatedly as she could (which usually meant short, meaningful sentences). Dena told her about her father's death and how their move to Brooklyn had been extremely hectic and how she was struggling at school and how money was becoming a huge issue for her single mother.

They decided to stop at a diner before heading home where Gio treated her to food. Dena insisted on paying but Gio said that she wanted to thank her for the day (and for the goals). Dena was surprised by the way Gio treated her and without a doubt she did not stop admiring Gio's neon green hair but it also caught her attention that Gio was wearing a t-shirt with a design by Andres, a famous characters designer.

"Is that a t-shirt designed by Andres?" Dena asked.

"Yes" – "Andres is my brother and he also designs sports teams and leagues logos" replied Gio.

Dena was surprised! Both girls continued munching on a hamburger and a bucket full of loaded fries and took short breaks in between to slurp on their oversized drinks. Both of the girls had an appetite. They shared a lively conversation over their food as they talked about their favorite leagues, teams, players, and everything that had to do with soccer. Dena could not help but feel invigorated as she was talking to someone about soccer after such a long time. This was a change of pace that she definitely needed.

After they were done eating, Gio suddenly paused and after taking some time to ponder over something, she said.

"Okay, you seem like a person who doesn't spill secrets, correct?"

"Yeah," agreed Dena, "I mean who would I tell?"

"Okay, great," replied Gio.

"So," she continued, "tell me then. Have you heard about the underground soccer league?"

Chapter Five

"The underground soccer league?"

Dena's curiosity was piqued as she voiced the question that lingered in her mind.

Geo's eyebrows shot up in disbelief.

"Wait, you seriously haven't heard about it?" she asked curiously.

"No," Dena admitted, shaking her head, "This is the first I'm hearing about it…"

A mischievous smile tugged at Gio's lips as she paused to take an exaggeratedly loud slurp of her drink. The way she guzzled it down without flinching raised Dena's eyebrows and stirred a mix of concern and amusement.

"How does this girl not have a chronic brain freeze problem?" Dena mused, half-smiling to herself.

"Okay," Gio said, leaning back and setting her drink aside before letting out a hearty belch, "I'll start from the beginning, but you have to promise to keep this to yourself."

"Again," Dena replied with a slight grin, "I really don't have anyone else to tell."

Gio stretched out, propping her feet up onto the sofa, and began to unravel the enigma of the mysterious underground soccer league.

The league had surfaced just a couple of years ago, but its rise had been meteoric, garnering a substantial following in record time. Throughout the state of New York, various teams had emerged representing different districts, and it was rumored that it was only a matter of time before the league went national. Currently, explained Gio, there were ten teams in New York as part of the league.

Technically, the league lacked any official affiliation with established soccer organizations. Its inception had been rooted in the simple desire for like-minded players to connect and compete. Officially, it was illicit—operating on the fringes of the law. Yet, legality mattered little in the face of passionate players and a rapt audience willing to pay a premium price to witness the matches. When people are willing to invest, the spectacle continues, rules or no rules.

The unorthodox nature of these games necessitated creative solutions for venues—for obvious reasons, they could not hold competitions on regular grounds. Over time, the league secured discreet locations for its matches. From repurposed airport runways to sprawling abandoned warehouses, these unconventional settings played host to fierce competitions that ignited the passions of players and fans alike.

But what set this league apart was its unique composition—entirely comprised of women soccer players. But all of these women were linked by a common thread. They were no ordinary players; they were outcasts, the very individuals society had discarded and dismissed as insignificant. They were the girls who bore the scars of bullying, rejection, and complicated family histories. Yet, in the face of adversity, they refused to be defined by their pasts.

Unlike succumbing to the vices that often ensnared their peers, such as alcohol and drugs, these women channeled their frustrations and sorrows into the beautiful game. The league provided an arena where they could channel their energy, and the fierce competition became a canvas for expressing their courage. Winning was paramount, not as mere validation, but as a defiant statement—a testament to their extraordinary skills, a declaration of their worthiness of recognition.

The intensity of these games often teetered on the edge of aggression. The driving force behind these players was not just personal glory but a collective mission to prove to society, their schools, and the established city leagues that had rejected them that they were exceptional, skilled athletes deserving of respect and admiration.

As Gio's words painted this vivid tapestry of determination and camaraderie, Dena couldn't help but be drawn into the realm of the underground soccer league. The narrative resonated deeply within her, touching the chords of her own past struggles and aspirations. In the shadows of legality, these women had forged a sisterhood, united by their shared journey of overcoming adversity through the sport they loved. And with each revelation, Dena felt a growing fire within her—a yearning to not only be a spectator but to become a part of this fiercely unyielding sisterhood.

"Anyways," Gio said, leaning back and exhaling a satisfied breath, "What do you think?"

Dena found herself at a loss for words, her mind still swirling from the cascade of revelations that had just flooded her senses. It was as if a hidden world had been unveiled before her, a world that was at once incredible and unbelievable.

Yet, despite the incredulity, Dena couldn't ignore the earnestness that radiated from Gio. She had a gut feeling that Gio wasn't the type to fabricate such a tale.

She blinked, processing the enormity of what she had just heard. This secret underground soccer league, an arena where outcasts transformed into warriors on the field, had now woven itself into her reality. As improbable as it seemed, she couldn't shake the feeling that it was indeed real.

"Okay, so," Dena began cautiously, her voice tinged with a mix of skepticism and curiosity, "Why did you even tell me any of this?"

It was a question that bore weight—a question that hovered between them like a mist, shrouding the true intentions behind Gio's revelation. Dena had only just met Gio a few hours ago; there was no logical reason for such a profound disclosure for unveiling a clandestine world that spanned the entire state.

Gio's lips curved into a playful grin, her gaze unwavering. "Well," she started, her tone both matter-of-fact and genuine, "Firstly, in case it's not already clear, I think you're very cool."

A blush crept onto Dena's cheeks, an involuntary reaction to the neon-green-haired girl's words. The idea that someone as distinct and unconventional as Gio could find her "cool" was both flattering and novel.

Gio's smile held a secret, a glimmer of anticipation that danced in her eyes. "And," she continued, her voice dipping slightly with mischief, "I plan on picking you up this evening and taking you to a trial match…"

Dena's eyes widened, a mix of surprise and disbelief settling over her. She couldn't help but question the authenticity of Gio's words. "You're kidding, right?" she ventured, a touch of skepticism lacing her tone.

Gio's response was swift and confident, her sly grin a testament to her unwavering intent. "No kidding," she assured, her words imbued with an air of authenticity that was hard to dismiss.

As Dena's mind whirled with questions about logistics, where they would go, and how this all worked, Gio dismissed her inquiries with a casual shrug. "Don't sweat the details," she advised, her voice tinged with a carefree assurance. "I'll fill you in on the way."

With that, the evening sun casting a warm glow on their conversation, Gio walked Dena back to her apartment. Just before departing, she turned with a wink that held the promise of adventure, of uncharted horizons. "Oh, and don't forget," she playfully reminded, "I'll be swinging by later this evening."

As Gio's figure receded down the street, Dena found herself standing at the threshold of an unknown journey. The promise of the evening hung in the air, intermingling with the echoes of the clandestine league that now existed at the fringes of her understanding.

In the midst of uncertainty, a new chapter was unfurling—a chapter that held the promise of camaraderie, competition, and perhaps a chance for Dena to weave her own story into the enigmatic tapestry of the underground soccer league. It all depended on how things would go down that evening.

True to her word, Gio swung by Dena's place that evening, punctuating her arrival with a resounding honk of her car horn. Dena met her with a mix of curiosity and anticipation, her heart beating a little faster as she stepped out and joined Gio. The setting sun cast long shadows on the pavement as they embarked on an adventure that held the promise of uncharted territories.

The evening breeze carried the whispers of a new beginning as Dena climbed into Gio's car. With a knowing smile, Gio revved the engine, and they set off toward a destiny waiting to be unraveled.

Their destination was a hidden gem in the heart of the city—a concealed field nestled away from prying eyes, a sanctuary for the spirited battles of the underground soccer league. To outsiders, it was just an abandoned warehouse.

As they arrived, Gio parked the car, and they trotted to the gate of the warehouse. A slit opened in the gate, and the dark eyes of a bouncer peered into Gio's. The gate opened and they went inside. Dena was dumbfounded at the instant change in scenery—the rickety exterior of the warehouse suddenly turned into a filly-equipped playing field.

Dena's gaze swept across the scene. The field was bathed in the warm glow of floodlights, a theater set for a drama that was about to unfold. But she did not have much time to look around since Gio rushed her to the benches where her team was waiting.

Gio's team, FC Brooklyn, faced off against their formidable rivals, Manhattan United. The tension was palpable in the air as the players took their positions. The energy crackled with anticipation, and Dena felt her pulse quicken in response.

From her vantage point in the benches, Dena's eyes danced over the players, recognizing a few familiar faces from her former school team that she had once played alongside. Her heart stirred as memories of practices and camaraderie flooded back. But there was something different about the atmosphere here—an intensity that transcended what she had experienced before.

As the match kicked off, Dena's attention was riveted to the field. The play was fast and furious, with tackles that bordered on the edge of what would be allowed in major leagues. The players' aggression was apparent, each move a testament to the stakes they were playing for. Dena's eyebrows furrowed, and she couldn't help but remark to herself that such rough play wouldn't be tolerated in more regulated games, but this made it even more exciting.

The game's crescendo built to a climax, a symphony of competition that resonated in every heartbeat. Despite their valiant efforts, FC Brooklyn found themselves grappling with defeat as the final whistle blew. The scoreboard might have reflected a loss, but the determination etched on their faces held the promise of a fierce rebound.

Dena watched as the players converged on the field, acknowledging the cheers of their fans. Among them, she spotted Gio, her face etched with a mixture of frustration and determination. As the players made their way to the sidelines, Gio's gaze met Dena's, and with a beckoning nod, she signaled for her to join them.

Feeling a mixture of trepidation and excitement, Dena walked down the bleachers and approached the team. Gio's introduction was met with welcoming smiles and nods of approval from the players. Each glance exchanged conveyed a message—of unity, resilience, and the unspoken understanding of what it meant to be a part of this sisterhood.

Once the introductions were done, Gio turned to Dena and asked her what she thought of the game. Dena could not hide how impressed she was.

"Okay, that's a relief," said Gio.

"What do you mean?" asked Dena curiously.

"I mean," continued Gio, "You wouldn't really play with a team if you don't like them, right?"

"Huh?" asked Dena as she tried to read between the lies.

Gio laughed and put one hand on Dena's shoulder as she explained herself.

"Don't you get it?" she said, "You might just be the missing piece. We need to tip the balance in our favor!"

Dena finally understood what she was hinting at. The gravity of the moment settled upon Dena's shoulders, the weight of a choice that held the potential to transform her life.

In this underground league, she saw both the wild thrill of competition and the haunting specter of the aggression that accompanied it. The stakes were high, the rules unorthodox, and the pressure immense. Yet, for the first time in a while, Dena felt a spark within her—an ember of hope and belonging that had been dormant for far too long.

As Dena stood amidst these fearless women, she recognized their stories in her own journey of resilience. A rollercoaster of emotions surged within her—fear and excitement entwined like a dance that beckoned her towards a path unknown.

It was a crossroads, a juncture where uncertainty met possibility. And in the midst of it all, Dena felt an unwavering conviction—she was ready to step onto the pitch and embrace the challenge, ready to chase after the exhilaration that soccer, camaraderie, and the underground league promised.

"So," asked Gio, "What do you say?"

Dena smiled defiantly.

"I'm in!"

Chapter Six

The roar of the crowd echoed in Dena's ears as she stood on the podium, a glittering trophy adorned in gold held aloft in her hands. Around her, her teammates surged with exuberance, their jubilation a chorus that seemed to shake the very ground beneath her feet. Their hands reached out, lifting her higher and higher, a testament to their shared achievement. Her name reverberated in the air, a mantra of triumph that seemed to echo for eternity.

"Dena!...Dena!...Dena!" they chanted.

Suddenly, Dena's eyes jolted open as a sharp pain rose from her forehead, making her realize how she had bumped it against her bedpost due to the exhilaration of her dream.

"DREAM!" she realized.

It was all a dream. But she could sense how real it felt as the remnants of the dream clung to her very skin. She was drenched in a sheen of sweat, and her heart was beating vigorously, reminding her of the rhythm of the chants. The vividness and weight of the trophy still lingered in her hands. She rubbed her eyes and felt the swollen blues under her eyelids. The late nights were definitely taking a toll on her skin.

The room was cast in the gentle glow of dawn, the world around her gradually waking from slumber. She flittered her eyes as they adjusted to the soft rays of morning sunlight tip-toeing through the curtain. She sighed as she looked around her tiny room. She had somehow managed to hang a poster of her favorite soccer team right on the wall in front of her bed. The players stared back at her, urging her every morning to get up and get done with the day so that she could focus more on her real passion—the one that hung on the wall.

She stared back at the poster for a while, and, with a heavy sigh, Dena shifted in her bed, her fingers brushing against the sheets as she tried to anchor herself in the present. The dream had offered a glimpse into a future where triumph was not just a fantasy, but a tangible reality— one that she was determined to chase. Every day since the first time Gio had taken her to visit the underground league, she had made it a routine to show up to the games after school. Gio wanted her to make her feel part of the team as well, even if she was not allowed to play for the time being.

She wanted her to study how they played and understand the team dynamics. She had always been good at analyzing games and it came to her attention that the FC Brooklyn was actually quite talented at creating a healthy, forward-pressing attack. They were skilled at creating openings, managing passes, and through-balls. Yet, the puzzle was incomplete. Dena recognized the missing piece—they lacked the finishing touch, that defining player who could seize the opportunity once the ball penetrated the adversary's penalty area. It was a role she had played in her dreams— the game changer, the one who could transform an opening into a triumph.

Gio's offer lingered in her mind like a beacon, a promise of possibility. If she dared to believe, she saw herself as that missing link. The thought ignited a quiet determination within her, a belief that she was meant to fill that void. With each passing day, the conviction grew stronger—that the team needed her as much as she needed them. She was perhaps the key that FC Brooklyn needed to get to the next level.

However, she was well aware that she was not going to get her spot right away. She would need to prove herself. And in order to prove herself, she would, first of all, need to show the team that she was willing to make sacrifices—that she was willing to show up to games even if she did not get to play. She knew that a forward person like Gio would be expecting commitment and responsibility from her and she was willing to do all it took to show her that she was ready.

With each passing game day, the anticipation grew like a crescendo. That fateful day arrived out of the blue—the qualifier match against the formidable Club Queens, a team that commanded respect in the underground league. The school day had passed in a blur; history lessons on the American Revolution, biology tests, and advanced trigonometry seemed distant echoes as her mind was consumed by the impending clash.

As the final bell rang, signaling the end of the school day, Dena's heart raced with excitement. Without a moment's delay, she raced back to the park where Gio and the team awaited her. The air was charged with anticipation, a symphony of nerves and determination interwoven.

The fierce competition awaited them—the Club Queens were no pushovers, a fact that intensified the significance of the match. Gio's encouraging smile greeted her as she joined the team. In that fleeting moment, Dena felt an unspoken camaraderie—the understanding that they were all in this together. The stadium lights cast a glow on the field, the tension palpable in the air. As the match kicked off, Dena's heart raced in tandem with her footfalls, the rhythm of the game synchronizing with her breath.

As the match's intensity unfurled on the field, Dena felt her pulse quicken in resonance. The symphony of pounding heartbeats, the rhythmic footfalls, and the collective breaths of players and spectators melded into an audible backdrop—a rhythm that mirrored the ebb and flow of the battle taking place.

Amidst this orchestrated chaos, a voice pierced through the clamor, a command that seemed both surreal and electrifying.

"Dena! You're up!"

The words reverberated in her ears, a symphony of urgency and opportunity that sent a jolt of surprise coursing through her veins. For a fleeting moment, she questioned if her imagination was playing tricks on her—a trick of wishful thinking that manifested her name being called. But then, the certainty of reality prevailed as Gio emerged from the sidelines, sprinting towards her with a fervor that matched the heartbeat of the game.

"Dena!" Gio's voice carried a fervent urgency as she reached her, eyes alight with determination. "Get up! We need you!"

Dena's heart raced, the echo of the command resonating within her like a clarion call. She felt her body respond instinctively, fueled by a mixture of shock and anticipation. The notion of being called onto the field felt surreal, as if she had suddenly been cast as the protagonist in her own narrative. A bewildered expression crossed her face, her mind grappling with the suddenness of it all.

"Wait," she uttered, a tinge of confusion lacing her voice, "Now?"

Gio's determination was unwavering, her words a rallying cry that brooked no hesitation.

"Yes, now!"

Her voice was a crescendo of urgency, an urgency that mirrored the gravity of the match that hung in the balance.

As Dena absorbed the weight of the situation, the gravity of the moment unraveled before her. The magnitude of being called upon to contribute to a pivotal game wasn't lost on her. This wasn't just another match; it was a moment that held the power to shape the team's destiny. It was now or never. She was hurriedly handed over a spare jersey and shoes that she quickly changed into and ran onto the field. She suddenly felt exposed. She felt like she was sitting in the middle of the school cafeteria where the eyes of all students, and teachers were directed at her, and all she could hear was the blaring rush of the crowd surrounding her.

But she knew that this was the moment she had been waiting for. The earth beneath her cleats seemed to vibrate with significance, every step a testament to the journey that had led her here. Amidst the backdrop of the ongoing match, her entry was a declaration—a declaration of her commitment, her readiness, and her willingness to embrace the challenge.

In that fleeting moment, as her feet touched the field and her teammates' encouragement echoed in the air, Dena felt a fusion of emotions—anticipation, exhilaration, and a sense of destiny intermingling. The game was far from over, but her presence was a catalyst, a catalyst that held the power to shift the momentum to transform the narrative.

With Gio's words still reverberating in her ears, Dena's gaze locked onto the pitch ahead, her focus unyielding. The opportunity had been seized, the challenge accepted. As she joined the ranks of her teammates, her heart swelled with purpose. In that pivotal instant, she wasn't just a spectator; she was a participant—a participant ready to inscribe her name in the annals of FC Brooklyn's history.

The sensation of the jersey against her body was a tangible reminder of the role she was stepping into—the embodiment of her connection with this extraordinary team. With a deep breath, she felt the adrenaline course through her veins, igniting a fire within her.

Her first touch of the ball was electric, a surge of familiarity and exhilaration that rippled through her body. Suddenly, she was in her element, her feet moving instinctively as she navigated the field. It was as if she had been reborn into a world where everything made sense, where every sprint and pivot was a declaration of her presence.

Her playstyle was dynamic all-encompassing. She was everywhere— defending with determination, passing with precision, and attacking with a relentless fervor. The crowd's cheers merged into a distant hum as the game played out like a symphony of coordinated chaos.

In a pivotal moment, Dena's instincts guided her, and she seized an opportunity. With a burst of speed, she surged forward, her feet dancing on the edge of the boundary line. And then, with a fluid motion, she struck the ball—a perfect arc that sailed into the net.

The eruption of cheers was thunderous, a testament to the significance of her goal. But there was no time to bask in the adulation. On the next play a player from the other team gave Dena an unpleasant welcome to the league with a very rude tackle. It was a reminder that in this league soccer is played not only with the heart, each game demands the maximum limit of strength and energy. With her heart pounding, she regrouped, rallying her teammates and orchestrating plays that flowed like a river. In a breathtaking sequence, she weaved through defenders, her footwork a mesmerizing dance. And then, with a deft touch, she sent a cross soaring towards a teammate who buried it into the net.

The old warehouse trembled with the resonance of triumph, the collective jubilation palpable. Dena's contributions had turned the tide, the match teetering on the brink of transformation. As the final whistle blew, FC Brooklyn emerged victorious, and their path into the group stage of the underground league championship trophy solidified.

Dena could not believe it. She had actually seized the moment. She had actually proven herself. She had actually managed to bring FC Brooklyn out of the trenches and into the glorious stages of the quarters. In the aftermath of the game, as the team congregated amidst an atmosphere of celebration, Gio's eyes met Dena's with a knowing gleam.

"We did it," she exclaimed, her voice a reflection of the shared victory.

Gio's words carried a promise, a whisper of greater things to come. As the team prepared to venture out to commemorate their achievement, she leaned in, her tone laced with possibility.

"Who knows, if we clinch that cup, we could be playing in the underground national league," she said as they headed out to celebrate.

Dena made sure to discreetly slip out of her FC Brooklyn jersey as she quietly entered her apartment that day. Her mom was soundly asleep in her bedroom but Lace (the family beagle) was ready to welcome her. The first thing she noticed was the pile of paperwork on the kitchen table. She instantly went over and organized these for her. These included some bills, school work, and other documents that Vera probably had to deal with after Frank's death. Dena sat on the kitchen counter and helped herself to a cup of water as she realized how she had not thought about her father for weeks.

She needed to figure something out about the situation at home. She could not just keep lying to Vera about her whereabouts. But knowing her, it was not entirely safe to tell her about the underground league either (although, in her heart, she desperately wanted to share this with her). Vera had still been struggling to adjust to the new place and all of the impending responsibilities that had landed on her shoulders. Dena was still trying her hardest to make sure that she helped her through all the household work and anything else she needed, but lately, with the underground league, it was getting harder and harder to play a more active role around the house.

She knew very well how Vera would react had she told her about the league. Ever Frank's death. Vera had become extremely protective of her. One time, she accidentally bruised herself on the ankle when they were moving their belongings into the apartment in Brooklyn and Vera started crying as she catered to the wound. Dena did not know how to react in that situation. She could tell that Vera did not wish to see her hurt or in danger in any way possible.

And so she decided it was best to keep this from her—for her own benefit.

Chapter Seven

On a cloudy Saturday morning Vera sighed.

It was a deep sigh of exoneration and relief. But the relief was masked with the dread of everything that awaited her. The tasks she faced might have seemed mundane to an outsider—laundry, grocery shopping, household cleaning—but collectively, they had started taking a toll on her ever since she had moved to Brooklyn more precisely since she had lost her husband.

In every little movement of hers, she could feel the absence of Frank. It was a lingering sensation on her skin, something that nagged and tickled against her receptors every once in a while, reminding her of what she used to have—a reminder of better times.

When Frank was around, she was still responsible for taking care of everything around the house. But back then, it was something she did willingly. It was something she found relaxing and therapeutic—like a job well done at the end of each day, a little pat on her back. For Vera, it had been a way of proving to herself that despite her disability, she was capable, strong, and self-sufficient. It had been her way of contributing, of finding solace in the routine.

Since Frank's passing, however, that once-therapeutic routine has morphed into a relentless burden. It was no longer a choice but an obligation that gnawed at her. The void he left behind echoed in every task, every movement, reminding her that her partner in life was no longer there to share the load.

Ever since his death, she had found herself questioning the strength that she once relied on over and over again. Could she really hold her own, she thought. Could she survive like this for potentially the rest of her life? Could she even survive like this for a couple more years until Dena eventually secured some footing in the real world?

The one thought that kept her going despite everything was undoubtedly Dena. Every time she thought of quitting, of ending it all, of disappearing and taking the burden of all the responsibilities off her shoulders, Dena's face flashed in front of her eyes. Those sad, beseeching eyes served as a poignant reminder that she had a daughter who relied on her unwavering strength. It was a silent pact they shared, an unspoken understanding that responsibilities could not be cast aside or evaded. They had to be confronted for the sake of their future. It was a constant reminder to her that she had a daughter to take care of. Reminding her that no matter how far she would run away, her responsibilities would eventually catch up to her one day. So, it was better to confront them rather than turn away.

As she slowly entered the apartment after a hard day's work at the school, her mind still heavy with the challenges of the day, she was met with a hungry Lace and with the sight of unwashed dishes in the sink—a tangible testament to the morning rush, where Dena had likely hurriedly prepared her breakfast before school. She sighed again, more resigned than exasperated, as she maneuvered her wheelchair to the sink's edge.

She gently twisted the nozzle on and methodically scraped the food from the dishes into the garbage can, washed them one by one, and watched as the gunk made its way into the void of the sink. What was once a routine that she deeply enjoyed had now become a constant source of annoyance.

Dena had been of great help when they had moved in. However, Vera had noticed lately how she was less and less available. It was the little things—the unclean dishes, the messy room, and how it had been ages since they had last sat down and had a proper conversation, mother to daughter. She had confronted her about this the night before, and Dena was very receptive but it felt as if her mind was still somewhere else.

What had led to her concern was the fact that in the past month or so. Every time she made it back home, she would not find Dena anywhere around the house. That was very unlike her daughter. Normally, Dena liked coming back early from school, playing with Lace, getting done with her homework, and taking care of other stuff around the house. But lately, her routine had entirely changed and without any explanation. She was not surprised by the latter, though. Growing up, she had placed an impeccable amount of trust on Dena's shoulders, and that naturally meant that Dena was extremely independent.

However, it still worried her, and she talked to her about it. As it turned out, Dena explained that she had made new friends and that she was really enjoying spending time with them. This was news because Vera was more than aware of all the troubles Dena had had to face back home due to her inability to make friends and the constant bullying. It was refreshing to hear that her daughter had found good company. She felt happy. Amidst all the chaos, her daughter was exhibiting signs of a healthy social life, which was an exhilarating development for her.

As she stood at the sink, Vera couldn't help but ponder the complexities of motherhood. Her daughter was growing, evolving, and finding her own path in the world—a path that sometimes veered away from the one Vera had envisioned. Yet, in the midst of all the uncertainties and changes, one truth remained constant: her love and concern for Dena, a bond that transcended the trials and tribulations of life.

She was almost lost in her thoughts and the rhythmic splash of water when her reverie was abruptly interrupted by the familiar sound of the door clicking open. She turned to find Dena strolling in with an easy smile, an effortless grace in her movements that seemed to radiate youth and vitality. Without a word, her daughter approached, greeting her with a warm hug that carried an unspoken reassurance.

Dena's presence was like a breath of fresh air, a testament to the resilience of youth. As she gently maneuvered her mother's wheelchair away from the sink, Vera couldn't help but smile inwardly. "Oh, to be young again," she mused, a fleeting thought that wafted through her mind like a soft breeze.

With a natural grace, Dena assumed control of the dishes, her hands moving swiftly and efficiently. Vera watched with a sense of maternal pride, her heart warmed by her daughter's newfound responsibility. It was a stark contrast to the burden Vera had felt earlier, replaced now with a sense of relief and gratitude.

While Dena worked, their interactions were marked by a comfortable silence, punctuated by the occasional question about Vera's day at school. Vera responded with small, genuine details, appreciating her daughter's interest and the ease with which they could share such moments.

As Dena seamlessly transitioned from the dishes to other household chores, Vera couldn't help but feel a sense of contentment. It was more than just the efficient handling of household tasks; it was the unspoken understanding that passed between them. The previous night's conversation had borne fruit, a testament to the respect and love they shared.

Despite the profound loss of Frank, Vera found solace in the fact that she still had someone to rely on, someone who understood her unspoken needs and was willing to shoulder some of the burdens. Dena's actions were a tangible reminder that they were a team, bound not only by blood but by the bonds of love and mutual support.

At that moment, as the domestic symphony of chores continued around them, Vera felt a renewed sense of hope. The challenges of her life were not insurmountable, not with a daughter like Dena by her side. It was a reminder that even in the face of adversity, they could find strength, resilience, and moments of quiet connection that reaffirmed the enduring power of their relationship.

The gentle rhythm of their evening routine was disrupted abruptly when Dena paused, her voice carrying an unexpected note of finality as she wished her mother goodnight. Vera blinked in surprise, caught off guard by the sudden end to their conversation. Fatigue must have been weighing heavily on her daughter, she reasoned, and she didn't want to press the matter.

"Goodnight," Vera replied, her tone carrying a touch of concern.

She watched as Dena moved towards their shared bedroom, gently closing the door behind her. The room fell into silence, the stillness punctuated only by the muted sounds of the apartment settling into nighttime calm.

Yet, as the door swung shut, Vera's eyes caught something that sent a subtle tremor of worry coursing through her. A reddish-blue bruise adorned Dena's shoulder, its presence like a silent alarm bell ringing in Vera's mind. She instantly remembered the second reason why she had been concerned about her daughter.

Over the past month or so, Vera had noticed a disconcerting pattern. In their brief encounters, Dena had often exhibited signs of minor injuries—bruises on her legs, complaints of sore shoulders, and back pains. While these injuries, in isolation, might not have raised alarm, their consistent recurrence had been a cause for unease.

Dena had always been meticulous and careful, especially in her sports activities, even back in their previous hometown. Her friends there shared the same cautious approach to play. This made the recent pattern of injuries all the more perplexing and disquieting.

Vera couldn't help but wonder if these injuries were linked to Dena's newfound social circle in Brooklyn. The worry nagged at her, tugging at her heartstrings. She knew she needed to address this growing concern, understand the source of Dena's injuries, and ensure her daughter's well-being in this new, unfamiliar city.

Chapter Eight

What Vera could not figure out was how she would bring up the conversation in front of Dena. How would she casually ask her that she had been noticing bruises and injuries all over her body?

It was not that the conversation was particularly difficult, it was just that Dena and Vera had not been the most conservative with each other in the past month or so and she thought that suddenly bringing up a heavy conversation like that might not be the best way to ease into it.

She woke up early that morning and was preparing breakfast. She had not done that in a while but she found her schedule to be relatively free that day which also made it a perfect time to have **the** conversation.

She thought about all the ways the conversation could go south as she flipped a couple of eggs on the sizzling pan. Meanwhile, she heard the door to Dena's room creak open slightly. Her daughter was up and was probably concerned about why the smell of eggs and bacon was coming from the kitchen.

She heard as Dena casually pushed the door open and walked out in her pajamas. She felt her rummage in the fridge as she grabbed a bottle of water and took a large gulp directly from the mouth of the bottle. She then put it back inside and walked behind Vera's shoulder as she peeked towards the stove.

"Smells good," she commented.

Vera smiled and Dena walked back to her room.

As she entered the room, she closed the door behind in a hurry. She felt agitated, thinking that her mom had woken up before her to make breakfast. Did she want to talk about something? Was there something on her mind?

She normally loved to tell Vera all about her day and everything that was going on in her life but she had lately been keeping a huge part of her life away from her and she had a feeling that it would blow up in her face any time soon.

She breathed out loud as she tried to calm her racing thoughts down. It was probably just going to be okay. Vera was probably just trying to do something nice. It definitely had been a while since she had eaten breakfast that she had made for her. It slightly reminded her of the old days—when everything was relatively normal in her life.

She changed out of her pajamas and hopped into the shower for a quick minute or so. Feeling the cold water run down her skin and dampen the slight reddish-blue bruises over her knees and legs felt slightly ticklish.

She stepped out of the shower and covered herself with her bathrobe. Entering back into the room, she quickly dried her hair and changed into her clothes for the day—a simple, plain white t-shirt and faded blue jeans with her trusted black Converse.

She stepped back into the tiny living room where the tantalizing smell of eggs and fried bacon on the table was everywhere and it made her mouth water. She instinctively sat down on the table and took a big bite of her food.

Vera smiled as she watched her daughter quite literally inhale all the food. She fiddled with her coffee cup as she thought of the best way to bring the conversation up. But she could not get herself to do that. Perhaps the image of Dena eating her hand-made food sparked memories in her head—memories of an easier time.

She wanted to stay in that moment for some time longer, for she knew all of it was fleeting by quite fast. And so, she watched Dena eat the food and decided against bringing up what she had been meaning to talk about.

She watched as Dena got up and thanked her for the breakfast with a wide, toothy smile on her face. Dena gave the last piece of bacon and toast to Lace and left the apartment, swinging her bag over her shoulder, happily whistling along.

Vera sighed as she watched her leave and decided to get ready for work as well. She ate quite little of what was left on the table, partly because she did not have much of an appetite and partly because Dena and Lace had pretty much devoured everything.

As she walked over to the school where she taught, she could not help but keep the thoughts out of her head. What was her daughter hiding from her? Why could she not just tell her? And why could she not just ask her? Why did she feel so disconnected from her own kin?

One of her colleagues, Angelica, must have noticed her distress. Vera was fiddling around with her routine coffee in the breakroom when she came in and decided to break the silence.

"Penny for your thoughts?" she asked in an endearing tone.

Angelica was a relatively older lady with three kids. She had graying hair on the edges of her forehead and one could tell looking at her that she was the sort of woman who had given up a lot to be where she was. She was one of the most experienced instructors at the school and she had a way with kids—and with adults, too, for that matter.

Vera smiled at her as she looked up and replied, "I'm okay…"

"Come on," implored Angelica, "Don't give me that. You know I can read through you, right?"

Vera sighed. There was no arguing her way out of this.

She told her everything that had been going on at home how she was concerned for her daughter, and how their relationship had been lately.

"It's not like anything is wrong between us," she explained, "But it's not the same as before either and I just wish there was a way I could get through to her…"

Angelica had a way about her where she would sit in front of a person and listen to them rant for as long as it took, without ever stopping to interrupt. She was like a human computer, taking in information and constantly making additions to her memory. But the way she interpreted that information was anything but computer-like.

When Vera was done with her tale, Angelica put her coffee mug down and weighed in on the situation.

She explained what she thought of the situation by telling her about her own kids and how she watched the three of them grow up and turn into adults. She was now seeing two of them off to college.

"So in my years of experience, dear," she said, "I have come to realize that you have to give your kids some space to figure out the people they wish to become. But they can't do that if you're over their heads all the time. You gotta give her some leverage here. As difficult as that sounds…"

"Okay…" continued Vera, "I hear you…but what about the bruises…"

"That," replied Angelica, "is definitely something to be concerned about. It is possible that a girl her age might just be getting bullied. But, on this one, you gotta reach out and ask her. Kids don't often feel the most comfortable telling their parents or teachers that they are getting bullied."

Vera realized she had not thought about that at all. In the constant struggle of trying to understand her changing relationship with Dena, she had completely forgotten to realize certain obvious possibilities. It had not occurred to her to ask her about her life at school.

She thanked Angelica as the bell rang, indicating the time for her next lecture. As she rolled out of the room, she kept getting this nagging sensation that it would be pointless to just straight up ask Dena about it. She needed to be sure.

"Maybe…" she thought, "Maybe if I can go to her room and see if something makes sense…"

She did not exactly like the idea of sneaking into her daughter's room but she felt extremely helpless. She remembered how Dena used to keep a diary when she was young. Maybe if she still did, she could get an idea of what to talk to her about. It was not the best plan and she knew that but she decided that she had to do something.

She left her job early that day, letting her supervisor know that she had some personal business to attend to. She was generally liked around the school, and she had a splendid work ethic, so it was not a huge issue for her to take some time off.

She reached home early that day, and naturally, Dena was nowhere to be found. She reached her door and very slowly turned the knob and rolled inside.

The room was a serious mess. It reeked of sweat and dirt and unwashed clothes that were lying all across the floor. Vera was genuinely surprised at her daughter's irresponsibility. She slightly forgot what she was supposed to do and instinctively went around picking up all the dirty clothes from the floor.

Something caught her eye all of a sudden.

"What is this…" she said out loud as she picked up a shiny purple jersey with Dena's name printed on the back of it. Vera didn't recall seeing a jersey like this. As far as she remembered, Dena always played in her old t-shirts and shorts back home, and if she had joined the soccer team at her school here, she would have mentioned something.

She flipped the jersey around and read out loud.

"FC Brooklyn?" she said confusingly.

Was her daughter in a local soccer team? Had she really been keeping this from her? Was this why she was covered in bruises? A thousand questions flooded through her mind. As she rummaged through the mess, she found a worn-out pair of soccer shoes covered in dirt and grass stains.

That night, as Dena sneakily entered the apartment, she was found by an unusual sight that made her gulp.

As soon as she opened the door, she was greeted by her used jersey and shoes lying on the living room sofa. Vera was sitting next to the sofa with her arms crossed. She had been waiting all this time for her daughter to come home.

"Care to explain?" she asked curtly.

"Uh oh," thought Dena.

Chapter Nine

"Care to explain," said Vera curtly.

Dena sighed. She thought about all the things she could have come up with on the spot. She thought about all the excuses she could have made. But when she stared into her mother's eyes and perceived the distant look of longing and anticipation, she could not get herself to lie.

She knew she had to come clean. And so she did. She was hoping that by at least being honest, Vera would see through her lies and appreciate her for confiding in her.

She told her all about the underground soccer league. She told her about how she had found a group of friends—Gio included—and how she had been going to secret matches with them all night long.

She explained why she had been coming home late every night and why she had been neglectful of small things such as her homework, her room, and the laundry. She filled her in on the bruises as well, which were just a marker of the tough games.

She also explained to her how she felt happy. How she had found a crowd, she finally felt a sense of belonging towards. She explained how the thrill and the exhilaration of the games helped her cope with everything that had gone sideways in her life.

She hoped Vera would understand. She hoped that amidst all the lies, she found a sense of purpose, of recollection, of her daughter's passion. But Vera reacted very differently to how she imagined.

She heard Dena speak for twenty minutes straight until she finally held her hand up in the air, motioning her to stop.

"So," she said in an exasperated tone.

"You're telling me…"

She rubbed her eyes lightly.

"…that while I have been out all day and all evening working to make ends meet…"

Her tone got sharper.

"…thinking that you were being bullied at school or something…"

Her eyes brimmed with anger and hurt.

"…you have been playing soccer at an underground **illegal** league…"

Dena did not know what to say.

"You understand how crazy that is, right? And straight up dangerous."

Vera finally could not hold it in any longer.

"DENA HOW COULD YOU HAVE BEEN SO IRRESPONSIBLE!"

"What do you mean?" said Dena annoyingly.

She could not understand why her reaction was so adverse. She was having fun, and she wanted Vera to support her in that aspect.

"Do you seriously not see the problem with this?" asked Vera.

Dena rolled her eyes.

"No," she replied, "Not really…"

"Dena!" she screamed, "You're playing in an illegal league where you could not only get hurt but could also go behind bars!"

"Come on," vented Dena, "Give me a break! No one is getting arrested."

"And how do you know that?" asked Vera.

"And you do you even care about me," she continued, "how could you even put me through this? Do you think I am not already having a hard time managing everything? Ever since your father…"

Her voice broke off.

She was silent for a while, so Dena decided to take that opportunity to sneak into her room.

"Oh, no!" yelled Vera, "Don't you dare try and close the door on my face, young lady!"

She rolled into her room.

"Ugh," muttered Dena, "Just leave me alone!"

Vera was taken aback.

"Fine," she said after a while, "But you are grounded. For a month! I want you to come straight home after school, and I don't want you anywhere around this Gio girl and that team…"

"That's so unfair…" protested Dena.

"It is what it is!" yelled Vera as she rolled out of the room, marking an end to the conversation. She closed the door behind her.

Dena's head was muffled under her pillows as the tears slowly cascaded from her eyes and dripped onto the bed sheet. The conversation with Vera played over and over again in her head. She had never heard her mother speak to her in that tone. She had never imagined she could speak to her in that tone.

She felt hurt and not-seen—which is the last thing she ever felt around Vera. Sure, she had lied. But it was for all the right reasons—she was trying to protect Vera all along. The last thing she wanted was for her to worry, and that is exactly what had led to her being grounded.

For some reason, her mind kept circulating back to her late father. Her Dad had always been her support when it came to soccer. She remembered when she was young, her Dad would take her to a nearby park, and she would carry a miniature ball in her hand to play with.

They would not talk much, but her Dad would keep passing the ball to her, and she would keep kicking it hard. He would have to walk all the way to the end of the park to constantly bring it back, but he would never complain—it was an unspoken bond between a daughter and a father.

It was through his encouragement that she first started playing soccer with her neighborhood kids. It was through his encouragement that she allowed it to become her passion, her source of peace.

It was his encouragement that solidified her dream of becoming a football star somewhere down the line. And now, as she lay crying on the bed, she realized that soccer was the only connection she had remaining to her father.

She suddenly felt her pillow vibrating, and she shuffled her hand inside to fish out her phone. It was Gio. She picked it up, and Gio instantly recognized that something was wrong. Dena tried to convince her that everything was okay, but hearing Gio's voice suddenly made her want to break down.

Before long, she found herself tearing up on the phone, and she recounted everything that happened with her mom to her. Gio was a patient listener.

"I'm here for you," she said, "Whatever you want…"

She explained to her how she was grounded. They had a big game that evening, so she had no idea how she would make it to that.

"Hey!" urged Gio, "Don't worry about it. If you can't make it, you can't make it. It's okay. Don't take too much stress…"

Dena thought about that for a while. She knew she was not okay with ditching the match. The only thing she wanted to do, in fact, was play for her team. In an instant, she made a decision that she knew she might end up regretting later.

"Okay…" she said, "Gio, can you pick me up in twenty minutes… discreetly…"

"Of course," she said as she cut the call.

Exactly twenty minutes later, she heard the quiet engine of Gio's car rumble outside her house. She was already ready, dressed in her entire kit. She quietly yanked her window open and walked into the fire escape.

She tiptoed downstairs, and as she reached close to the ground, she jumped and rolled onto the grass. She took one final look at her apartment and sighed as she turned and walked over to Gio's car and slid inside.

"Let's go," is all she said.

Chapter Ten

As the night settled over the city, Dena's heart raced with excitement and trepidation. Gio drove like a maniac but Dena could barely focus on her swerving through the lanes because her mind kept wandering back to the image of Vera. Part of her felt terrible that she lied to her. This was also the first time she had done anything as rebellious as sneaking out of her window while being grounded. But she also felt angry and hurt.

Regardless of everything, she also knew the importance of the upcoming game for FC Brooklyn. It was a match that could determine whether they would advance to the coveted quarter-finals of the underground league. Despite the late hour and everything that went off at home, she couldn't shake off the urge to play, to make a difference. She just wished Vera could see it in the same light as her.

"If she cannot understand," thought Dena, "Then it's fine. I am going to keep my secret world hidden from her. Whatever it takes."

But there was more to it than that. She could not just suddenly disappear from a crucial game because she had become a regular member of FC Brookly—a crucial part of the team's fabric. The camaraderie she shared with her teammates, many of whom had faced similar struggles in life, was a source of strength. They were more than just a soccer team; they were a tight-knit family, bound by their love for the game and their determination to prove themselves.

She was not willing to give that up for anything. In fact, it was the first time in her life that she felt that she actually had a family outside of her house. But she had to shove all of this out of her head for now because they had reached the venue. Much like always, it seemed to be an abandoned warehouse from the outside but as soon as Dena stepped outside into the cold night, she could feel the electric energy of the crown inside buzzing through the air.

They went inside and they were not surprised to find the stadium buzzing with energy, the crowd's fervor a tangible force on the field. Both Gio and Dena joined right after the half-time point. The game hung in the balance, with FC Brooklyn needing a remarkable comeback to secure their spot in the quarter-finals. Dena, with her unwavering determination and unyielding spirit, became the catalyst for this transformation.

As soon as she touched the field, everything started to connect. The passes, the through balls, the shoots—everything made sense. Her life suddenly had an urgent feel of semblance. The passes soon turned into dribbles and her immaculate footwork led her directly into the enemy territory. But no one was going to stop her from scoring that night. In fact, she scored not just one, but three goals in a matter of twenty minutes.

Her hat-trick was a testament to her prowess, a display of raw talent and unrelenting resolve. With each goal, the crowd roared in approval, the noise echoing in her ears like a powerful affirmation. Her teammates rallied around her, inspired by her remarkable performance. It was a turning point in the game, a moment when the odds shifted in their favor.

As the final whistle blew, the scoreboard confirmed their victory. FC Brooklyn had done the unthinkable, and Dena had been their guiding star. Her hat trick had not only secured their place in the quarter-finals but had also cemented her status as a hero in the underground league. It was a moment of triumph, a celebration of her indomitable spirit, and a glimpse of the bright future that awaited her in the world of soccer.

Her team raised her up on their shoulders and chanted her name out loud. The feeling of belonging, of worth, and of pride was unreal. It was all remarkable until she caught a glimpse of a familiar face sitting near the entrance of the warehouse, staring directly at her.

Vera glanced at her daughter from her wheelchair, her arms crossed, and her expression curt. Gio sensed something was wrong and, as she followed Dena's eyes, it did not take her long to realize that they were both staring at Dena's mother.

"Uh…okay guys," she said, "Put her down, please…"

"Yeah," Dena said hurriedly, "I gotta go…"

As she started to walk towards her mother, Gio grabbed her hand from behind and whispered in her ear.

"If anything goes wrong," she said, "Let me know…"

Dena nodded in response.

As Dena approached her mother, the joyous atmosphere began to dissipate, replaced by a storm of emotions. Vera's expression revealed everything. There was a huge mask of hurt all over her. She could not believe that her precious daughter had lied to her and went right back to doing the one thing that she had told her not to do.

More than that, she felt disrespected and concerned.

Their argument was heated, voices rising in discord as they stood at the crossroads of their opposing views.

Vera's voice quivered with worry and desperation. "Dena, you can't keep doing this. You know how dangerous it is. Your safety... it's all I think about."

Dena, caught between her dreams and her mother's fears, tried to reassure her. "Mom, it's not that dangerous. I'm careful, and the team needs me. This is my chance to shine."

Their words clashed like opposing forces, neither willing to concede ground. Dena's dreams and Vera's maternal instincts clashed in a tumultuous battle.

As people walked past them in the parking lot outside the warehouse, they sent occasional glances at the mother-daughter duo as their voices rose to higher decibels.

"What do you mean it's not dangerous?" screamed Vera, "We are literally standing outside an abandoned warehouse. What part of this screams safety to you, huh?"

Dena could see the point she was trying to make but she would do anything to not agree with her.

"I know you probably hate me for this…" continued Vera, "But I am doing this because I know what's best for you…"

Dena could not take it anymore. She went off, and her voice rose higher than Vera had ever seen before.

"YOU DO NOT KNOW WHAT IS BEST FOR ME!" she screamed.

"IF YOU DID, YOU WOULD NOT BE HAVING THIS CONVERSATION WITH ME RIGHT NOW!"

She said something then, which pierced through Vera's heart.

"Stop acting like you know me!"

Vera's breaths suddenly became shallow and rapid. Panic gripped her, and she clutched the arms of her wheelchair, her knuckles turning white. Dena, once blinded by her determination, suddenly saw her mother's frailty in stark relief.

In that moment, as her mother began to have a panic attack, Dena felt the weight of her defiance. She realized the fragility of Vera's condition and the toll her actions were taking on her mother's health. The memory of losing one parent was still fresh, and the thought of losing another, especially due to her own actions, was unbearable.

Dena rushed to Vera's side, as her own eyes filled with tears. "Mom, I'm so sorry!"

Her voice quivered with regret.

"I'm here. Please, let's just go home."

In the midst of their conflict, Dena's love for her mother prevailed. She couldn't bear to see Vera suffer, knowing that her actions were causing her pain. It was a turning point, a moment of clarity, and a decision made out of love and responsibility.

"Gio!" she screamed as Vera struggled to catch her breath.

"We need help here!"

Gio was about to leave when she suddenly heard Dena's voice from the other end of the parking lot. She rushed to her side only to realize that she was holding a trembling Vera in her hands.

"I'm here," she said hurriedly.

Gio and Dena managed to roll Vera into her car and they headed off.

"Should we go to the hospital?" asked Gio as she eyed Dena from the rear-view mirror. Dena had her arm wrapped around Vera, who was breathing in short and sharp intervals, taking in every breath as if the very act of breathing was sending sharp tings of pain soaring across her lungs.

Dena was getting increasingly worried about her mother's condition. She had never seen her have a panic attack before, and the very sight of it was making her lose her mind.

"Yeah," she replied in panic, "I think we should go to the hospital…"

"No…" groaned Vera weakily from under the cover of her hands.

"Just take me home," she continued, "I'll be fine…"

"Mom, please let us take you to the hospital. It's fine…"

"Please," interrupted Vera, "Just take me home for now…"

Both Gio and Dena knew better than to argue. She turned the car around at the nearest intersection and headed for Dena's place.

Little by little, Vera felt herself reconnecting with her senses as her breathing slowed back down and her heart stopped beating as ferociously as it was before and eased into a more gentle rhythm.

"It's going to be okay, Mom," she heard Dena's gentle voice.

Chapter Eleven

The following days passed in a blur of anxiety and convalescence. Vera was recovering at home, her MS condition compounded by a severe bout of flu and anxiety that had sent her health into a tailspin. Both mother and daughter decided to temporarily put their respective schedules on hold, their focus entirely on the path to recovery.

Vera, her usually resilient spirit temporarily dimmed, spent most of her days in bed, a high fever casting a shroud of discomfort over her. On the bedside table lay rows of medications, a necessary but unwelcome companion in her battle against illness.

Dena, filled with a sense of guilt and responsibility, made it her mission to ensure that her mother followed the strict regimen of pills and treatments prescribed by the doctors. She monitored the clock with unwavering determination, making sure that each medication was taken at the scheduled time. Feeding her mother became a ritual of love, a slow and patient process of coaxing nourishment into Vera's fragile form. Nausea and illness may have reduced her appetite, but Dena knew the importance of sustenance in her mother's recovery.

Despite the challenging circumstances, Dena's relentless care and unwavering love played a crucial role in helping Vera regain some of her strength. Day by day, the fever began to recede, and Vera's resilience slowly began to shine through the cloud of her ailments.

Amidst the day-to-day challenges, Gio's desire to visit was appreciated, but Dena couldn't help but feel that it might be best for Vera to remain shielded from her secret life. The recent health scare had been a stark reminder of the fragility of Vera's condition, and they both agreed to take things slow in revealing Dena's clandestine activities to her mother. The priority was Vera's recovery, and they were willing to put all else on hold until she was back on her feet.

She wanted to talk to her really bad about everything that had happened recently between them. She wanted to open up and tell her everything. She wanted to tell her how it had all started, how she had found a crowd she finally felt accepted in. She wanted to tell her about all the games they had played, all the injuries and small bruises she had suffered, and how she had become an extremely valuable member of the team.

But she also knew that it was best for Vera if she steered clear of that topic. In all honesty, she did not know what was best for her exactly, but she was doing all she could to make sure her mother felt okay— physically at least. Every once in a while, she would give her massages, change her bed sheets, and bring her fresh clothes to wear. On top of that, she also had to take more responsibility around the house. Making sure everything was spick and span, taking care of Lace, that there was food in the fridge, that the bills were in order, everything was on her shoulders for the time being.

The initial days of taking care of her mother had been challenging, but Dena was quick to adapt to the responsibility. Her temporary break from school allowed her to focus on Vera's recovery and ensure that every medication and meal was attended to with meticulous care. The routine gradually became less of a burden and more of a purpose, a way to express her love and concern.

Yet, as Dena settled into this new role, she couldn't help but feel a growing void in her life. She missed her soccer team, the thrill of the game, and the camaraderie with her friends. She knew that they were still out there, playing their matches and chasing their dreams, while she was confined to her home.

As much as she tried to avoid the conversation about her secret life, it was inevitable. Vera, who had been visibly recovering, decided that it was time to address the elephant in the room. Dena sensed the impending conversation lurking in the silence, a weight that hung between them until one day, it couldn't be avoided any longer.

Towards the end of the week, Vera started feeling relatively better. She was moving around more and was becoming more active physically.

That evening, out of nowhere, Vera invited Dena to her room, a hint of resolution in her eyes as she asked her daughter to sit down on the bed next to her. The atmosphere was heavy with unspoken words, and Dena knew exactly what her mother wanted to discuss.

"You know what I want to talk to you about," Vera began, her voice gentle but firm. Dena, with sheepish eyes, looked back at her, a mixture of anticipation and apprehension in her gaze.

"Tell me everything," Vera said, her tone laced with concern and curiosity.

And so, with a deep breath, Dena began to recount her secret life, her underground soccer league, and her unrelenting passion for the game. It was a conversation that had long been postponed, but now it unfolded between mother and daughter, a moment of truth and vulnerability. Dena shared her dreams and desires, her longing for the field, and her fierce determination to make her mark in the world of soccer.

At first, she only provided Vera with the overarching details. However, as the conversation progressed, she realized there was no longer any need to keep her deepest feelings and experiences hidden. The floodgates of emotions opened, and tears streamed down her face as she spoke of her journey since their move to Brooklyn and how the loss of her father had taken a heavy toll on her young heart.

Dena admitted that she had never truly processed the grief of losing her father. She had been too preoccupied with the chaos that had enveloped their lives since then. Soccer, she confessed, was her sanctuary, a place where she felt like she truly belonged. The game had become her escape, her passion, and her dream.

Vera listened, her own eyes glistening with unshed tears. She understood her daughter's pain and longing, and she knew the role soccer played in Dena's life. With a heavy heart, she said, "You have to understand my concerns."

Dena nodded, her voice trembling as she replied, "I do understand your concerns, and I get it."

Vera held back her tears, her maternal instincts warring with her knowledge of what might be best for her daughter. "I know you're right, and I know you've been trying really hard to keep things balanced here while I'm out playing soccer."

Dena sighed, torn between her love for the game and her love for her mother. "Don't worry, I won't go back."

Vera couldn't believe the words coming from her daughter's lips. She sensed the inner turmoil, the conflict between Dena's desires and her responsibilities. "Is that a promise?" she asked.

With a deep breath, Dena replied, "Yes," her words carrying the weight of sacrifice and love. It was a promise made to her mother, a testament to her unwavering devotion.

As Dena lay on her bed, her mind in a whirlwind of thoughts and emotions, she couldn't help but ponder the conversation she had just had with her mother. The weight of her promise to Vera and the sacrifice it entailed bore heavily on her heart. While she knew she had done the right thing, her love for soccer and her friends tugged at her emotions.

Aunt Fer had been in the other room, checking up on Vera. She had known Dena since she was a baby, and they had shared a close bond.

However, their interactions had dwindled recently due to Dena's secret soccer activities.

A light knock on her door, and the subsequent appearance of Aunt Fer didn't surprise her. She had likely heard about the conversation with Vera and wanted to offer her perspective. Dena straightened up on her bed as she entered and sat on the edge, facing her.

After some small talk, Aunt Fer began to express her thoughts. She acknowledged Vera's concerns but also sympathized with Dena. Unexpectedly, she didn't launch into a lecture about safety and responsibility as she had anticipated. Instead, she voiced his belief that Dena shouldn't completely abandon her friends and the game.

Dena, bewildered by his words, asked, "What do you mean?"

Aunt Fer continued, "I think you should at least play through the finals, even if your mom disagrees. Your friends might need you."

Dena hesitated, torn between her promise to her mother and her longing for the game.

Aunt Fer, however, had another idea. "Even if you're not playing, you should at least go and encourage your friends, cheer them on. It's better than sitting here cooped up like this."

Dena was concerned about leaving her mother alone, but Aunt Fer assured her, "Don't worry about that. I'm here with her."

Realizing the opportunity, Dena asked, "You mean I should go right now?"

Aunt Fer replied, "Yes, go support your friends! Is there a match going on right now?"

Dena nodded, "Yeah, we're playing in the quarters."

Aunt Fer encouraged her, "Then why are you still sitting here? Go support your friends!"

Dena was taken aback by her unexpected advice, but she felt a renewed sense of purpose. She jumped up, ready to head to the match. "Are you serious?" she asked, seeking confirmation.

Aunt Fer smiled, "Absolutely. Go! And don't worry, I'm here with Vera."

Chapter Twelve

"We barely made it to the semi-finals today, Dena…"

The manager had called Dena aside post-game to have a small discussion with her. Mr. Pata was an old, burly figure who always had a pointed hat on his head, which accentuated his figure.

Despite his intimidating physique, he was actually a very sweet and caring man who always made sure that the girls on his team had everything they needed to excel on the field and outside of it as well. This is why he was also really understanding when Dena told him about how things were slightly chaotic back at her place.

"I understand that things are really bad for you, dear. But you saw the match today. You understand that we really do need someone to take up the striking department, right? The girls are looking good this year, but we desperately need someone to finish the game…"

Dena nodded in agreement. There was not much she could say, considering how she had already promised Vera that she would not play in the league again.

"We made it to the semis on nothing but luck, honestly…" he continued.

"That might be a slight exaggeration," thought Dena.

"…so I really need you to rethink this whole thing. Talk to your mom and try to make her see what you see, okay?"

"I'll think about it," she said as she left the arena that night.

The team was slightly tense as they met outside the arena at a nearby park. They could barely get themselves to enjoy or celebrate anything, considering how they had won after playing a neck-to-neck game. They knew luck would not always be on their side, which is why they were getting increasingly concerned about the semi-finals, where they needed to rely solely on their ability to maneuver the game rather than abstract things like luck.

They were all extremely dismayed by the fact that Dena was not on the field. All of them had made a strong connection to the girl, not just in their emotional life but also on the field. They understood her position as a striker really well, and they had all grown used to her playing style to the point that they had shifted the team strategy in such a way that the entire game revolved around making sure that passes were circulated enough to eventually reach Dena in the hope that she would finish off with a score. Her absence left a void in their tactical approach, and they were unsure of how to adapt without her familiar presence.

Dena could feel the tension in the air as she sat with them in the park. Gio started off by discussing the strategy for the semi-finals. She could not help but appreciate the command that Gio had over the team and the conviction with which she spoke. More than that, she could not be more in debt to her for being a kind-hearted friend throughout all this time. She had understood Dena's situation and had stuck with her, never forcing her to play when she did not want to—she had prioritized their friendship over the game itself, and Dena could not respect anything more.

Later on, she pulled her aside and asked her to update her regarding everything.

"Mr. Pata is being really pushy, honestly," said Gio as Dena recounted everything that had happened the past week to her.

"No," she replied, "He is right. But there is nothing I can really do about this, you know?"

"Yeah," replied Gio, "I understand. You know I do."

Dena, however, was determined about one thing. Even though she couldn't join her teammates on the field, she was determined to support them wholeheartedly. She had given her word to her mom, but she also couldn't bear the thought of staying away from the arena during the semifinals. The passion and camaraderie she had developed with her teammates were too strong to resist. Thus, she decided that, despite the promises made to her mother, she would be in the arena the following evening to cheer her fellow teammates on during the pivotal semifinal match. Her heart was with her team, and she couldn't stay away when they needed her presence the most.

The following evening, Dena realized that sneaking out was not as easy as it sounded on paper. Then again, she realized that it was Gio who always helped her do it, and now she was on her own since Gio was busy with the game. Vera was asleep in the adjacent room.

There was no way Dena was going to go through the subway at night. She did not wish to be ambushed by strangers. She decided to go the expensive route and call an Uber instead.

She was hoping for the driver to discreetly arrive at the front door of the apartment building, but luck really was not on her side. As soon as she quietly clicked the door shut, she heard the immense and unrelenting honking of the Uber from down below, and by that point, she had no option but to make a run for it.

It was the constant honking that woke her up. There were not a lot of cars in the neighborhood where they lived, so Vera was really surprised when she heard blaring noises coming from the front gate of the apartment.

She yawned as her body slowly started to wake up, and she rolled outside into the living room to get a glass of water. That is when she realized that the door of the apartment was slightly open, and so was Dena's room door. She peered inside only to realize that her daughter was nowhere to be found. Adding two and two together, it only took her a second to realize that it was she who had forgotten to lock the gate as she hurriedly sneaked outside.

It took her even less than that to know exactly where her daughter had gone off to.

Disappointment clouded her face as she grabbed her coat, ready to head back to the arena.

"KEEP IT MOVING!"

"PASS! PASS! PASS!"

"KEEP THE SHOW MOVING! COME ON! DON'T STOP MOVING THE BALL!"

"THAT'S IT!"

"NO, THAT'S NOT IT!"

"COME ON GIRLS. WE GOT THIS!"

Dena was screaming her lungs out from the stands. She did not care if the girls could hear her or not, but she wanted to make sure that she was as present in the game as she could be, even if she was merely spectating from the sides.

Gio had not joined the game yet and she was warming up on the benches, but even she had stopped giving instructions, considering how Dena was already doing half the job for her. Neither team had scored a single goal, and the game was edging close to half-time.

Technically, Dena had kept true to her promise. Vera could not help but agree to that as she saw her daughter sitting in the stands, closely watching the game. However, what took her by surprise was the fact that the person she was looking at did not seem like her daughter at all.

It was almost as if, within that arena, Dena was an entirely new person altogether. She saw a new energy radiate from her as she screamed her heart out, giving directions and making sure that her friends were on the right track in the game.

"Who was she?" thought Vera.

And then the realization struck her. The realization that had taken a long time to arrive. The realization was that they had been clouded by everything that had happened ever since they had moved to Brooklyn. Vera's vision was no longer clouded, and, like an epiphany, everything hit her at once.

"That is my daughter!" she thought as it rained down on her.

Chapter Thirteen

The crowd's fervor echoed through the stadium, a symphony of cheers and chants that reverberated in the air. Dena was caught up in the electric atmosphere, her eyes fixed on the intense soccer match unfolding on the field. The stadium buzzed with an energy that seemed to seep into every pore of the night. Colors blended into a kaleidoscope, cheers merged into a symphony, and amid this vibrant chaos, Dena found herself immersed in the world of soccer, her sanctuary within the stands.

She was blissfully unaware of the approaching revelation.

The distant echoes of the crowd were suddenly accompanied by a closer sound, the gentle shuffle of someone approaching. Dena, engrossed in the game, felt an intrusion into her private soccer haven. When she turned, expecting to find some fervent fan, her gaze met her mother's eyes—eyes that held not a reprimand but an understanding that sent shockwaves through Dena's emotional defenses.

Vera stood there, a soft, understanding smile playing on her lips. It was a gesture that defied the scolding Dena had braced herself for. The stadium's ambient noise seemed to muffle, leaving a moment suspended between mother and daughter, a moment where words hovered, waiting to be spoken.

Dena felt the world shifting beneath her feet. She felt the ground slip as she realized how she had been caught. She had been caught at the one place she promised not to go back to. Her throat suddenly felt dry as she thought of the right words to utter. But before she could say anything, Vera surprised her.

"You're not in trouble, sweetheart," Vera's voice cut through the buzz, her words gentle but resonating over the chorus of the crowd. "I see you found your place here. But maybe it's time to join your friends on the field. You belong there just as much as you do here."

Dena could not believe the words she was hearing. Was this really her mother speaking?

Dena's initial shock transitioned into a cocktail of emotions. Confusion, relief, gratitude—all swirled within her like a whirlwind. Caught off guard by the warmth in Vera's words, she tried to find her voice amidst the inner cacophony.

"But... Mom," Dena began, her voice a hesitant whisper amid the stadium's roars. "I promised you I wouldn't play."

Vera's smile persisted as a beacon of understanding in the tumult. "Sweetheart, promises are important. But so is finding your place, your joy. I've seen how much this means to you. Maybe it's time to redefine that promise."

A pause hung between them, pregnant with unspoken sentiments. Dena felt a surge of conflicting emotions like a river finding a new course. The stadium, with its rhythmic heartbeat and kaleidoscope of emotions, bore witness to this transformative exchange between mother and daughter.

"Go, Dena," Vera encouraged, her eyes reflecting a newfound clarity. "Join your friends on the field. Be where you belong."

In that moment, the soccer-filled air became the backdrop for a profound understanding, a bridge mended, and a connection renewed.

The stadium roared in approval, unknowingly celebrating not just a game won but a relationship rediscovered.

Before Dena could fully absorb the unexpected turn of events, her arm was seized in a firm grip, the touch familiar yet urgent. She turned to find Gio, her neon-green hair a beacon in the stadium's colorful chaos. She had apparently heard the entire conversation.

"Okay, girl," Gio exclaimed in a hurried whisper, "We need you. We need to beat Manhattan United! Go change! GO! GO! GO! No time to lose!"

Caught in the whirlwind of Gio's urgency, Dena nodded, her mind a blur of conflicting emotions. She hurriedly made her way to the changing rooms, the ambient sounds of the stadium morphing into a distant hum. The air in the locker room buzzed with anticipation as Dena, in her FC Brooklyn jersey, felt the weight of expectation settle on her shoulders.

In a flash, she changed into her soccer gear, the familiar routine a comforting anchor amid the storm of emotions. The cheers from the crowd outside reached a crescendo as word spread that Dena, the talismanic striker, was making a return.

As Dena emerged from the changing room, the cheers intensified. Her teammates, recognizing the significance of the moment, rallied around her. The camaraderie in their eyes mirrored the crowd's acknowledgment of her presence. Dena, both humbled and invigorated by the support, felt a surge of determination. She sprinted towards the field, her heart pounding in sync with the stadium's roar.

On the sidelines, Vera, initially taken aback by the whirlwind unfolding before her, watched her daughter with a mixture of pride and concern. The soccer field, a space where Dena found solace and camaraderie, suddenly became a battlefield where her daughter's choices played out in real-time. The applause from the crowd, once a distant murmur, now echoed in her ears, and Vera couldn't help but be moved by the realization that her daughter had carved a place for herself in this dynamic world.

On the field, tension hung thick in the air. The scoreboard displayed an equal score, a testament to the fierce competition. The 80th minute loomed, a critical juncture in the game. Dena, now amidst her teammates, felt the weight of their collective hopes.

The referee's whistle pierced the charged atmosphere, signaling the resumption of the game. Dena, her focus unwavering, positioned herself on the field. The next few moments would not only determine the outcome of the game but would also be a defining chapter in Dena's journey.

The game resumed with an intensity that seemed to reverberate through the stadium. The opponents, aware of Dena's return, marked her closely, determined to keep the star striker from influencing the game. But Dena, fueled by a newfound energy and the unwavering support of her teammates, weaved through the defensive line with grace and determination.

The minutes ticked away, each pass, each tackle, a strategic dance on the field. Dena faced relentless challenges, defenders converging on her with calculated aggression. Yet, she pressed on, her dribbles and passes contributing to the ebb and flow of the game.

As the clock inched towards the 90th minute, the tension reached a fever pitch. The scoreboard remained deadlocked, the outcome hanging in the balance. Dena, with beads of sweat glistening on her forehead, sensed the collective heartbeat of her team. The opposing goalkeeper, vigilant and focused, mirrored her determination.

In a final surge of adrenaline, Dena received a precision pass just outside the penalty box. The defenders closed in, but with a swift move, she evaded their tackles. The crowd, sensing a decisive moment, erupted in cheers. The goalkeeper, a formidable obstacle, eyed Dena with steely resolve.

Time seemed to slow as Dena wound up for the shot. The ball, a sphere of dreams and aspirations, connected with her foot. In that fleeting moment, the stadium held its breath. The net rippled as the ball found its mark, a resounding goal that echoed triumph.

The referee's whistle pierced the air, signaling the end of the match. The stadium erupted in jubilation as FC Brooklyn secured victory against their rivals, Manhattan United!, in the dying moments. Dena, amidst the cheers of her teammates and the thunderous applause of the crowd, felt a profound sense of accomplishment. Her journey, marked by challenges and choices, had led to this victorious crescendo on the soccer field.

Dena, the hero of the moment, found herself hoisted onto the shoulders of her jubilant teammates. The camaraderie and joy radiated from the tightly knit group as they carried her in a triumphant procession across the field.

Cheers and chants enveloped the stadium as the victorious team paraded Dena, the architect of their success. The elation was palpable and contagious, spreading through the players and the spectators alike. The once tense and competitive arena transformed into a spectacle of unbridled celebration.

Amidst the sea of exuberance, Dena, perched high above the crowd, could hardly believe the scene unfolding below. The teammates who had become her second family, the supporters who had witnessed the highs and lows of their journey, all joined in the jubilation. The resonance of their victory echoed in every cheer, every clap, as they reveled in the shared triumph.

In the midst of this euphoria, Vera, watching from the stands, felt a swell of pride and relief. The apprehensions and concerns that had clouded her perception of Dena's soccer pursuits seemed to dissipate in the joyous air. Seeing her daughter embraced by friends carried on a wave of celebration, Vera's heart swelled with a mixture of maternal pride and a newfound understanding.

The stadium became a canvas of pure joy, painted with the vibrant hues of victory. Dena's journey, marked by challenges and choices, had culminated in this moment of shared glory, and Vera, despite her initial reservations, couldn't help but share in the infectious joy that echoed through the stadium. FC Brooklyn received the champion's trophy designed by the famous artist Andres (Gio's Brother).

Mr. Pata, the team manager, announced that the team qualified for the US national championship. A man (Patrick "Duck" – The US National Team Coach) approached Dena and Gio to inform them that they were selected by the US national team to compete in the Underground World Cup in Madrid, Spain.

www.ingramcontent.com/pod-product-compliance
Lightning Source LLC
Chambersburg PA
CBHW071439300726
48976CB00004B/1386